LAND · HC

STORIES FROM THE SISKIYOUS

Ursula Bendix

Ursula Bendix

Memoir
BOOKS
Chico, CA

Land · Home · Mountain View

STORIES FROM THE SISKIYOUS

Copyright © 2020 by Ursula Bendix
ISBN: 978-1-937748-30-2 paperback
ISBN: 978-1-937748-31-2 epub

Library of Congress Control Number: 2019952129
First Edition

Memoir Books
An Imprint of Heidelberg Graphics
Chico, California 95928

Photos: Ursula Bendix

I want to thank my teacher, mentor, and friend Jacalyn McNamara who helped and encouraged me in the long process of writing and completing this small collection of stories. I also thank my children, Nika and Peter, for supporting me in this endeavor.

CONTENTS

PROLOGUE

A VOYEUR

Watching two people exchange mutual physical pleasure and thereby enjoying vicarious sensual arousal is named voyeurism. Watching two people exchange kind and thoughtful actions is considered, however, observation of human nature. Yet, isn't all observation a type of voyeurism whereby the observer encounters a set of external actions from which he/she experiences some pleasure or discomfort not of his/her own making?

Following this line of thinking, Ingrid Fromm unabashedly

considered herself a voyeur as her eyes and thoughts followed a young couple leaving the spa of this quaint mountain resort to which she retreated from time to time. From the deck of her rented cabin, she observed that they had left the bath-house wrapped in only the blue and white striped resort tow-els. *Odd, most people dress before exiting the bathhouse. Maybe they're going to change when they reach their cabin. Maybe they're just day guests and changing rooms had all been occupied.*

Her usual trips to the mineral springs were for the day only—just long enough to take a hike up a logging road to a clearing where she could sit and view the towering image of Mt. Shasta, a mere twenty-five miles to the south, followed by a return to the bathhouse for an excruciatingly hot mineral bath, an exhausting stay in the sauna, capped off by a frigid shower. She never dipped into the spa's icy pool, formed by the damming of the mountain creek, that added such charm to the ambiance of the resort. Many spa regulars preferred the arctic chill of the pool to the more controllable temperature of the showers, claiming that submerging themselves in the nude was extremely beneficial for the body's internal organs. If time permitted, she would wrap herself in the cotton sheet provided each guest, recline on a deck chair, and sun for a while before driving leisurely back home. The added benefit to this routine was a deep, restorative sleep.

On this visit, she decided to treat herself to an overnight stay. Her mobile phone was turned off, she didn't recognize any of the guests—she was anonymous and unacknowledged. This was a pleasant change from the frequently hectic days guiding, explaining, answering, and defusing questions and problems arising from real estate buyers and sellers in the busy brokerage firm she co-owned. What a luxury!

The young couple was walking away from the bathhouse.

Each was carrying a backpack in which, Ingrid assumed, they had stored their clothes. They stopped in the middle of the covered walking bridge leading over the roaring Parks Creek whose water provided the icy cold contrast to the heat of the sauna. Although the resort proprietors had published a warning that the 38 degree water temperature might not be healthy for everyone, Ingrid was almost positive these two had jumped *au natural* into the creek after each session in the sauna.

They set their backpacks down and turned slightly in her direction. She recognized them from the previous afternoon's sweat lodge organized by the Native American community for the benefit of all who felt the need to cleanse their spirit. These sweat lodge events were sporadic, she was always happy when her visit to the resort coincided. The beating of the drums, the chanting of ancient feelings accompanied by the sounds of the rushing creek brought magic to the resort's setting among the tall, fragrant pines of the surrounding hills.

She recalled the heat and smell of the sweat lodge, but her attention even then had been the young couple. They passed a water bottle back and forth and with each pass had looked at one another calmly and gently. The slow, deliberate offering of water was always anticipated by the other, without word or touch. *Was this a demonstration of being in sync, being in complete and absolute harmony of thought?*

It was this perceived harmony that again drew Ingrid to observe the young couple in the middle of the bridge. *How is it possible to be so in tune with another person to be able to anticipate the other's wants and needs? Was this intimacy?* For several years now, she had wondered about the meaning of intimacy, what it is and how it is attained. It was not physical intimacy she questioned, but the intimacy of the spirit. *Is intimacy an abandonment of the self? Is intimacy indistinguishable from affection? Can two people ever truly be intimate in spirit?*

The Spanish speaker uses the term "tener confianza" to imply trust between two people when they can speak freely, however, the term does not go so far as to mean an intimacy of spirit. The English speaker uses the words "soul mates" to emphasize two people ideally suited, but do these words suggest an intimacy of spirit or only a compatible set of values?

Her thirty-four-year marriage ended in divorce. The process toward this end had been like the slow release of air in a balloon, an undetected pinprick, until it was deflated. Voyeurism, she knew, was a means by which she tried to discover and comprehend the nature of intimacy. She was sure that once she understood this feeling, she would understand the essence of living.

Since she couldn't hear them, she watched their movements intently—two mimes giving an exclusive performance. The young man stepped slowly behind the young woman as she began to remove her towel. He took both ends of it in his hands, encircling her body with his arms and the cloth, leaving just enough room for her to pull on a longish, tie-dyed skirt first and then a sleeveless bright turquoise blouse, both of which she had previously taken from her bag and laid at her feet. As she bent down to retrieve each article of clothing, he would also move down, making sure that the towel covered her. He averted his eyes and turned his head to look at the creek. He resembled a tango dancer stepping slowly in rhythm with his partner. Once dressed, she stepped forward, he opened his lose embrace, guided the towel away with one hand, then folded it before handing it to her. He had shielded and protected her.

Perhaps an integral part of intimacy is protecting and shielding. Ingrid tried to remember if her husband, her mother, her father, or anyone had protected or shielded her as an adult. Her husband would say, "You can handle that, you're strong." Her mother's comment, "Just pay attention to what you're doing." Her father's unwavering refrain, "I think you know what you should do." But, of course, she didn't always know and didn't always pay attention and wasn't always strong. She needed their protection, their affection.

Now it was the young woman's turn to guard him against all possible onlookers. As he loosened his towel, she gracefully stepped in front of him, extending her arms slowly and carefully to take hold of the ends. She also averted her eyes, turning her head, as he had, toward the creek as he sidled into his trousers. *Why this delicacy? They surely are familiar with each other. Perhaps it demonstrates a public protection of their intimacy.* A look from him and she swayed to his side releasing her hold on the towel. The towel dropped. She bowed to retrieve it, folded it before offering it to him. As if choreographed, they picked up their backpacks in unison, filling each with their shield—the now-folded blue and white towels—and slowly finished their walk across the bridge, hand in hand.

And she, the voyeur, sat still for a long time after the couple's departure, bathed in the gently exchange of intimacy.

CHAPTER 1

WHY WOULD A GROWN MAN...?

Siskiyou County, California, over three hundred miles north of San Francisco, is the true Northern California. Forty-five thousand people comprise the entire population in an area the size of Rhode Island and Connecticut combined. You can get lost here, stake out your territory, and retreat to a lifestyle reminiscent of rugged individualism and grit, and pre-mobile phone connectedness. In fact, mobile phones are useless in much of the county crisscrossed as it is by the Siskiyou Mountains, the Marble Mountains, the Trinity Alps, Mt. Shasta, the Eddies, Black Butte, and the long canyons formed by the Sacramento, Klamath, Shasta, and Scott rivers.

Following his discharge from the Veterans Hospital in White City, Oregon, Bob Smith traveled around southwestern Oregon a bit, renting a room here and there, but never settling into place for any length of time. The often foggy and overcast winter sky in this region of Oregon depressed him, and so, he decided that sunny California might be the solution to his restlessness. He drove the short distance from Medford, Oregon, over the Siskiyou Summit into California, arriving in an area called the Klamath River Country Estates. There he found a mobile home on 2.5 acres to his liking and bought it.

He soon acquired a couple of dogs to keep him company. In the evenings, he would sit on his porch and listen to the coyotes howl as they closed in on a kill. His dogs would rush to his side and quiver. The wildness of the area intimidated them, but pleased Bob. After three tours in Vietnam where silence in the forest meant the enemy was near, he welcomed the nightly howls and hoots.

On his weekly visits to town, he would stock up on food and refreshments and then, before heading home, stop at the Log Cabin Saloon. Tall tales were told there of man-eating mountain lions, sleep-deprived brown and black bears, and coyotes the size and meanness of wolves. With a few drinks in him, he would join the banter at the bar. He would start talking about the ugliness of his missions in Vietnam, the gruesome details of legs and arms flying in the air. The more he talked, the more his companions edged away. For the young men at the bar, the Vietnam War was as remote as World War II. There was no collective memory of anti-war rallies and protests. Soon he would be sitting at the bar by himself, sad and morose, not the happy drunk with tales of wild game-hunting prowess that would have been more welcome.

He stopped going to the saloons in town and took liquor home with him—sat on his deck drinking and listening to the sounds of the night. Extreme loneliness took hold, and he realized that something needed to change. Once again, he set out to town in the evenings. This time he decided to try another bar, one that, from the outside anyway, appeared a little more high class.

On one of these visits, he noticed a middle-aged woman sitting at the bar by herself. He thought he had seen her there before, but wasn't sure. She looked pleasant enough, with short hair, a bit thick around the middle, and just a little too stout from behind, but not too much makeup. Bob didn't like women to wear much makeup. He had avoided the Vietnamese girls in the Saigon bars all made up, giving out favors; he felt sorry for them.

The woman at the bar seemed quite ordinary and even approachable. Luckily for him, there was a seat open next to her as he sauntered up to order another beer.

"Mind if I sit here?" he asked in as natural a tone of voice as he could muster.

"No, it's still a free country."

"Sometimes I wonder! I'm Bob. You here a lot?"

"Oh, once in a while when I get tired of watching TV by myself."

"Me too. Hell, it's sure hard to meet people in this country. No one wants to hear about the war, that's for sure."

"What war are you talking about?"

" 'Nam."

"You mean Vietnam? That's too long gone. Even I don't remember that much about it. My son's in Afghanistan right now—should be comin' home in about six months. I worry about him all the time."

"Hey, can I buy you another drink? I won't talk about 'Nam."

"Sure."

And so the friendship between Bob Smith and Linda Walker began. At first they would meet only at the bar, later on he would come to her house and watch TV and help with minor repairs. When the weather got warmer, they would take long drives along Highway 96 which followed the Klamath River. They would stop here and there to try their luck at gold panning. Bob didn't have much patience with the slow and meticulous process of twirling the water and sand around the inside of the grooved mining pan. He would either go too fast so that the sand and water could not separate or too slow, preventing the heavier particles from being washed up and settling into the grooves of the pan. He would soon give up, sit back, and smoke a cigarette. He couldn't understand how Linda was able to sit for hours at the river's edge, slowly turning the mining pan this way and that way, even though she never saw "color."

Sleepovers did happen on occasion, but only because it wasn't safe for him to drive home. For Bob, the attachment was immediate. Life became tolerable.

"Bob, Brian's comin' home. He wants me to pick 'im up at the Medford airport next Tuesday."

"I'll drive you up."

"Don't get me wrong, but I want to meet him alone. It's

been such a long time."

"Sure. Hell, I just thought maybe the two of you could talk better if I did the drivin'."

"Thanks, but I've been lookin' forward to this for so long. We'll all get together later in the week."

"Where's he goin' to live? Is he gettin' a job?"

"With me of course. What a silly question! Jobs are hard to find right now. I just want him to relax and settle in again."

"Call me if you change your mind—glad to drive."

"Sure. I'll call once things get settled down."

But Linda didn't call. He went back to some of his old habits—drinking one beer after another, mindlessly watching old movies on TV, or sitting out on the front porch of his mobile home staring at the hills and listening to the night sounds of animals shifting about. He waited the entire week before breaking down and calling her. Later, he wished he would have waited for her call. Maybe it would have turned out better.

The night he called, Brian the son answered the phone.

"Can I talk to Linda?"

"Who's this?"

"Never mind who this is—let me talk to Linda."

"Are you okay, mister?"

"Hell, yeah. Just let me talk to Linda."

"Okay, okay. I'll get her."

"Is that you, Bob? Are you drunk?"

"Hell right I'm drunk. You haven't called me."

"I told you I'd call as soon as things got settled down."

"How long's that take? How long's he goin' to stay with you?"

"As long as he wants to stay—Bob, don't call me again unless you're sober," was her last remark to him as she hung up the phone.

He felt humiliated and alone. *Why would a grown man want to live with his mother?* His heart was broken. He tried to understand how happy Linda was to have her son back safe and sound, but his loneliness and longing for companionship engulfed his spirit. *It just isn't right!*

The only way out was to sell his place and move on. He called the office of the agent who had sold him the property, but that agent was no longer selling real estate. Some of the other agents he contacted didn't want a listing that far out of town. He finally managed to find an agent willing to come and look at his place.

"Would 2:00 p.m. be okay for us to meet at my office?" asked Ingrid after getting some of the preliminary information.

"No, before noon's better."

"How about eleven o'clock?

"That'll work."

At precisely eleven o'clock the following morning, Bob Smith walked into the real estate office. He looked somewhat bewildered. He couldn't remember the agent's name—Yvonne, Inga—he was reluctant to ask.

Since she was expecting him, Ingrid came forward to greet him, "I'm Ingrid Fromm and you must be Bob Smith, right?"

"That's me."

"Come, let's go to my desk and fill out some of the forms I need before I come out to take pictures and put up a sign."

Ingrid watched his hands. They shook a little as he completed and signed the listing papers. When he looked up, his eyes were red-rimmed and a little watery. She had seen this before, but couldn't quite remember where and under what circumstance.

"Bob, I have tomorrow afternoon free to come out. Late afternoon is best for me. I'll be able to go directly home after that."

"No, afternoons don't work out so good. Anyways, it gets too hot by then. 10:00 or 11:00 in the morning works best for me."

"In that case, I won't be able to come until Friday."

"That's okay. No big hurry."

Driving through the Klamath River Country Estates to meet Bob on Friday, Ingrid listened to Patsy Cline's doleful sounds. She found this to be very relaxing. Country western music suited this place. There were no fences or No Tres-passing signs—just miles of yellow grass and indigo blue sky. This huge country subdivision, consisting of five thousand acres of rolling hills filled with juniper trees, scrub oaks, and chaparral, had been divided into various sized parcels.

Most were small, about 2.5 acres, but adequate enough to accommodate a well and septic system. Some of the roads through the subdivision were paved but the majority just dirt and gravel. In the summer they were dusty and wash-boarded and in the winter muddy and almost impassable.

Located about thirty minutes northeast of Yreka, the county seat, the KRCE was established in the 1960s when there was still a lot of logging, ranching, and gold mining available and people were moving into the county. Here it didn't take much money to set up a little ranchette and be free from city building restrictions. The county had few building requirements—the ground had to percolate to sustain a septic system and there had to be a constant source of water. Electricity was not necessary, a generator was sufficient—no curbs, sidewalks, or gutters were required either.

The area attracted the individualist, the hate-to-follow-the-rules type, who believed building codes were just another form of the government telling everyone what is best. The subdivision had a slightly disheveled look. Manufactured homes, mobile homes, trailers, and "stick" built homes intermingled without order or consistency. What, somehow, brought harmony to all of this was the outrageously beautiful setting of snowcapped mountains, silhouettes of grand oaks on steep slopes, and a sea of hills rolling as far as the eye could see.

The foothills of the Siskiyou Mountains, the wide open spaces, and the dramatic vistas were pleasing to the eye. It was easy to understand how someone could imagine that a place such as this offered peace and freedom from society's demands. *Who would find you in these hills?*

Bob's place was at the farthest reaches of the subdivision. Ingrid would have liked to have ended her workday after this visit, drive through the car wash in town, and go home. Another agent might have been more adamant, insisted that the late afternoon was the only time available, but Ingrid didn't have the heart. By now she intuited Bob's concern about afternoon appointments.

He and the two dogs were waiting for her at the front door. He showed her the outside sheds, helped her measure the perimeter of the mobile, and then took her inside. As she stepped into the mobile, she collided with a dark smell. At first, she thought it might be the odor his dogs left behind. But it was more than that. It reminded her of the heavy musty smell that comes from bars when a door is left open on a hot and windless day.

The blinds were closed against the morning sun, keeping the rooms cool as long as possible. Once her eyes had adjusted to the darkened rooms, she could see that there was little in the way of furniture—a sofa, a couple of lounge chairs, a coffee table, a kitchen table, two chairs, some electric appliances on the kitchen counters—not much else, but sufficient for one person. Several large posters of John Wayne hung on the living room walls. And, to her surprise, everything was neat and orderly if not completely dust free.

As she was leaving, he asked, "Why would a grown man want to live with his mother?"

Ingrid didn't quite know how to respond, but then ventured, "Maybe he doesn't have any other place to go. Maybe he doesn't have any money, or maybe he just likes living there."

"Yeah, but a grown man shouldn't be livin' with his mom. Hell, at eighteen, I was on my own."

"Bob, maybe he hasn't grown up yet."

"You'd think the service would've made a man out of 'im."

"Can I ask you who you are talking about?"

"My girlfriend's son come back home—looks like he's there to stay."

"Maybe he's just there until he figures out what to do."

"Hell, I haven't seen her since he's been back."

"Why don't you call and ask her out to dinner? Then you wouldn't have him around."

"Hell, she won't talk to me no more."

"Maybe she's not the one for you. It's hard to make a break, but sometimes that's the only thing to do."

Ingrid did not like talking on such a personal level with her clients. She felt that her private life and the private lives of her clients shouldn't mix. Selling and buying property was complicated enough without all of that. She wondered what she would do if her son Alex came back home to live. He was home for a couple of weeks before starting a new semester. *No need to think about this now!* Right now she was planning his favorite meal—crepes filled with strawberries and topped with whipped cream.

At about 9:00 p.m. the phone rang. Ingrid and Alex had just settled down to their favorite "hospital" series on TV. Alex was in medical school and liked to laugh at the improbable situations on the show.

"Why would a grown man want to live with his mother?" *Oh dear, sounds like he has had too much to drink.*

"Gosh Bob, I really don't know. Why don't you call your friend? Don't say anything about her son and just invite her out to dinner or take her on a Sunday drive. Tell her how much you miss her. Forget about her son."

"She bought him a new truck. Hell, I drove by the house and there it sat. The sticker's still on."

"Bob, he might have bought the truck with money he saved from his army pay," Ingrid responded half-heartedly. "I'm sorry about all of that, but I'm really not the right person to talk to about any of this. I took Psychology 101 in college, but that just confused me. I'll call you if there is someone who wants to see your house. Take care."

"Mom, who was that?" Alex called out.

"Just a client with a personal problem."

"All of your clients tend to have personal problems," he remarked without looking away from the television set.

Bob called every evening from then on, and every time he would ask the same question, "Why would a grown man want to live with his mother?" Every evening she would try to give him a rational answer and tell him that she was not the best person to consult about this. And every evening Alex told her not to make her clients' problems her own.

Unfortunately, the market for mobile homes on country acreage had declined. Lenders were no longer giving loans for mobiles without engineered foundations, and without loans the buyer would have to pay cash, or the seller would have to carry a note. Also contributing to this flat market was the escalation of gasoline prices which had buyers looking for property closer to town and their jobs. In any case, these little faraway properties lingered on the market.

Bob's evening calls became more desperate. Linda had never returned any of his calls. The son's new truck continued to be parked in the driveway. He just couldn't understand why the son was still at home and how Linda put up with that.

On the last evening of Alex's visit, he had gone out to celebrate with friends who were also home for the semester break from their respective colleges. She hoped that their high school habit of appointing a designated driver for such "celebrations" still applied. When he was at school, she didn't worry, but now that he was again under her care, the old worries returned. She didn't allow herself to sleep until she heard him come in.

The phone rang. Thank goodness she knew her son was home, otherwise it would have frightened her.

"My truck's broke down. I need a ride."

"Bob, is that you? Where are you?"

"Front of the Log Cabin Saloon. Sorry. Sure as hell can't call Linda."

"Okay, I'll be there in about twenty minutes."

Why did I say I would get him? That drive out there is awful in the dark, and what if he gets sick in the car? What'll I do?

"Alex, wake up. You're going to have to help me drive a client home."

"Mom, are you crazy? Can't you just say no to these people? Why can't he just sleep it off in his truck, car, or whatever?"

"I guess that's a problem I have. It's probably too cold, even at this time of year, for him to sleep in his truck. You know how cold it gets at this elevation when the sun goes down. Well if you don't want to, I'll go by myself."

"Okay, okay. I'll come, but don't expect me to talk."

"Thanks."

They picked him up at the tavern. Ingrid got out of the car to introduce the two men. Her son also got out, intending to open the back door for Bob. Bob attempted to get into the front, but Ingrid's son blocked his path. When she introduced the two, neither extended a hand. They grunted at each other, slid into their seats—Alex in front and Bob in back. No one spoke during the almost thirty-minute drive. Ingrid couldn't tell if Bob was sleeping in the back seat or if he was just sadly quiet or angry. Her son fell asleep in the front seat. True to his word, he didn't speak the entire time Bob was in the car.

Driving through the dark expanse of the subdivision with only her headlights to guide her, she occasionally looked up at the star-filled sky. She could make out the Big Dipper, and she spotted Venus shining as brightly as ever. She recalled a scene from the movie *2001: A Space Odyssey* in which the spaceship was floating through space to the music of a Strauss waltz. The noiseless ship, moving ever deeper into the Milky Way, gave the impression of impending mystery and drama. She imagined her vehicle to be a spaceship with two bodies lying asleep in time capsules programmed to not wake up until a destination was reached, and she, the humanized robot, in charge of the journey.

"Bob, wake up! Are you okay?"

"What's the matter? Hell, where 'm I?"

"You're home. Alex and I drove you out here. Can you get out by yourself?"

"Yeah, I can get out," he responded in a somewhat testy tone. "Sorry you dragged your son out. Would've been okay just me 'n' you."

She watched him struggle with the seatbelt, but was afraid to help. That accomplished, he turned to open the door. "Where's the damn door handle? Never mind, I got it."

Slowly, he lumbered out of the car. Ingrid wished her son would rouse himself to help. He didn't.

"Bob, I am going to try to get you in contact with someone at the VA hospital either in White City or in Sacramento. I'll call you with the information. If you need a ride to get your truck, I'll be happy to drive you into town sometime in the morning in the next couple of days.

"Yeah, thanks."

And so she left him at the front porch of his mobile and watched him as he wobbled up the stairs. His dogs had been waiting for him. Before getting back into her car, she looked up at the sky. How absolutely beautiful! There were no sounds coming from the dark expanse of land, all was quiet on this "Western Front." *It's going to be okay. He will move away from here and forget all about Linda and her son.*

At a distance from the mobile, her son woke up. In his most exasperated voice, he intoned, "Mom, you've got to stop getting involved. There's nothing you can do for him. You said that it was almost impossible to sell his mobile right now."

"I'm going to call Behavioral Health tomorrow. Maybe they can call him directly and give him some advice."

"Just leave it alone! You're not *his* mother or his girl-friend."

"Alex, a little compassion is necessary in life. I hope you remember that when you're a doctor."

She took him to the airport in the morning. His last re-proach was, "Mom, just let people figure out how to solve their problems. You're a real estate agent, not a counselor."

"I'll try to remember that. Take good care of yourself and study hard. We need good doctors."

Ingrid was sure her son would not come home to live with her. She could tell from his confident stride as he passed through the terminal, not once looking back, he was walking toward a life very separate from hers.

Maybe compassion is something that comes with more expe-rience and less self-assurance. Maybe a doctor's self-assurance is more important than his compassion. Maybe, in some special cases, self-assurance and compassion come together.

Now that she was free from her son's disapproval, she called some of the agencies she thought might be able to help Bob—Behavioral Health in Yreka, VA hospital in White City. Each promised to call him.

When she finally called Bob to again extend her offer to drive him into town to retrieve his truck, he told her he had already taken care of that. He didn't need her help. He had decided not to sell his property and when it was convenient for her, she should come and get her signs.

Oh well—so much for trying to help!

Bob and his problems faded as she went about her daily office routine, answered telephone inquiries, and reviewed the numerous forms in each transaction file. Ingrid's last call of the day came just as she was shutting down her computer and straightening her desk.

"My name is Nina Mazzola. I'm looking for an agent who can help me sell my house in Hornbrook."

"Sure. I'm Ingrid Fromm. I do work that area. When would you like me to come out and take a look?"

"Tomorrow morning would be fine. And by the way, are you allergic to ferrets?"

CHAPTER 2

NINA

Hornbrook, a hamlet of fewer than 300 inhabitants in Northern California, has the appearance of neglect. Poverty and desolation are evident everywhere. When driving through town to show a property, Ingrid always notices the similarity with the poor Andean towns in South America where she had worked as a Peace Corps Volunteer so many years before— stray dogs barking, chickens crossing the road here and there, some raggedy looking children sitting on porches, dark and strangely dressed teenagers milling around aimlessly. And just like those towns a continent away, Hornbrook has spectacular scenery. Not the snow capped Andes, but the rugged, forested hills of the Siskiyou Mountains with Mt. Shasta in the distance acting like an anchor to the world that makes living here tolerable.

Ingrid Fromm tried to time property showings in Hornbrook for late afternoons or early evenings. It is at these twilight hours that the hills to the east radiate such lovely shades of pink and purple as the western hills begin hiding the sun. Leaving Hornbrook she would take the county road home following the Klamath River, cross the Klamathon Bridge, then head south along Ager Road. Mt. Shasta would emerge once she passed Black Mountain. As the eastern hills turn pink, so do Mt. Shasta's snow and ice fields.

When her son was very young, he would say, "Mom, look at the mountain! Mt. Shasta is pink."

And she would reply, "Alex, that's called 'alpenglow.'"

Until he left for college, whenever they were together and the mountain turned pink they would repeat this dialogue, getting some strange satisfaction from this exchange.

Ingrid became acquainted with Nina Mazzola when Nina decided to sell her property in Hornbrook. She had bought the house on one acre with Cottonwood Creek frontage only two years prior for what seemed, at the time, coming from San Francisco, an unbelievably low price. She had a little money and a lot of time, and this property was exactly what she thought she needed. With just a few paid-for-renovations, and some elbow grease on her part, she'd have a perfectly lovely home.

The idea had been to get away from the city, the grime and polluted air, grow her own vegetables, and begin the healing process her body required. Two radical mastectomies, an earlier hysterectomy, increasing joint stiffness, and high cholesterol levels convinced her that her only hope for survival was a complete change in lifestyle.

The slow, clean, uncomplicated country life was what she needed. She'd done research on the internet and identified the area just south of the Oregon/California border as possessing most of her criteria—an altitude of 2,500 feet for the optimum level of oxygen in the air; at least one hundred miles inland so as not to be subject to damp sea air or a possible tsunami; most importantly, there could be no industry that might emit toxins.

Having identified Siskiyou County as an area with most of the essential elements for a clean, toxic-free life, she began to narrow down the areas within the county she liked best and the least expensive. Hornbrook, Siskiyou County, California, at the required elevation and geography, having little business and no industry of any type, became the location for Nina Francisca Mazzola's new life.

A bonus of the area was the Buddhist temple Tashi Choling in the nearby settlement of Hilt. This solid-looking building with its red tiled roof, nestled against the side of a hill looking south toward Mt. Shasta, inspired peace and tranquility. She would be able to visit the temple for meditation and Buddhist study sessions. These activities, coupled with pesticide-free vegetables from her own garden, clean air, and less stress would help rejuvenate her body and spirit.

The house Nina bought required renovation. The initial dollar investment, however, was little compared to the money she needed to change this charming run-down cottage into the environmentally friendly home she had envisioned. Her extra money soon disappeared. Loans became necessary.

The day she walked into the real estate office in neighboring Yreka, only Ingrid Fromm was present.

"I want to sell my house. What do I have to do?"

"Where is the house?"

"It's in Hornbrook. Are you familiar with Hornbrook?"

Oh no, not Hornbrook! "Yes I am."

"Well then, let's get started. I don't want this to take too long because I plan to move to Africa. More precisely, I want to move to Ethiopia."

From the frying pan into the fire, huh? "Okay then, the sooner we get the listing papers together, the sooner you can move on," was Ingrid's somewhat tepid response.

To Ingrid, Nina's raised eyebrows and direct look implied—this agent will have to do. I have to move on. I need to get this over with.

On a dusty Tuesday afternoon, Ingrid pulled into Nina's property. The driveway was hidden by an array of overgrown shrubs. She would have passed it had her eyes not caught the huge arrow with house numbers painted on the stucco wall of the neighboring trailer park pointing to its entrance.

She got a sinking feeling—bushes and small trees amid the tall pines—so much vegetation. She could hear Cottonwood Creek, but not see it. If inside of the house was anything like the outside, she knew this would be a difficult property to sell. *Life is full of difficulties. You just have to persevere.*

Ingrid gingerly stepped on the broken pavers leading to the front door. She knocked. "Come on in, the door isn't locked." Ingrid was about to enter when she heard Nina's now, somewhat-frantic voice, "Quick, close the door. I forgot to put the ferrets away."

Oh, my, gosh! What am I going to do if one of them attacks me? She saw a couple of tails sticking out from under the sofa.

Why didn't she put them away? People with antisocial tendencies let their animals run havoc.

Nina appeared with two ferrets attached to her body, one on each shoulder. "Have you seen ferrets before?"

"No, I always thought they were illegal as domestic pets in California," Ingrid replied.

Nina gave her a look that clearly meant to say—what does that matter? They amuse me.

"Nina, I'll just go outside and look around until you've rounded up all the ferrets."

"Just be careful where you step. I haven't had a chance to clean up after the dogs—don't try to pet any of the cats. I got this hideous scratch from the calico the other day. It still hasn't healed."

This will definitely be a challenge! I should just walk away, make up some excuse, leave, pronto! But she couldn't do it. She wasn't sure that she approved of Nina or that Nina thought much of her, but once committed to a project, Ingrid could not turn back. She sensed that Nina needed help. Perhaps there was just enough about Nina that Ingrid admired. Nina, from what Ingrid could see, had totally disregarded the practical, something that she, Ingrid, could never do.

The tour inside the house left Ingrid dismayed. The ferrets had taken over. In the kitchen there were tubes constructed of cloth and netting everywhere—slides and rope ladders for these creatures hung here and there. The laundry room was totally devoted to padded cloth cages and more tubes through which the ferrets could scurry and play.

The garage and several storage rooms had been converted to bedrooms or bathrooms. Into each of these conversions, Nina had installed a separate heating system. Nothing was finished—uneven floors, molding around the windows not replaced, closet doors missing, stained carpets, paint color samples smeared on the walls. *What a nightmare!* But most peculiar of all was what Ingrid saw in Nina's bedroom closet.

The closet was huge. It might have been a separate room at one time. Hanging neatly were several rows of identical outfits—a type of velour running suit in every imaginable color. In a few of the colors, there were two or three duplicates. Below the suits stood, as if waiting to be jumped into, sneakers of matching color.

In other rooms, stacked against the walls, were piles of half-wrapped framed photographs. "Nina, are you a professional photographer?"

"No, I just like taking pictures and then frame them. It's my hobby."

Ingrid wished she could see what Nina liked to photograph. An opportunity would present itself.

Once the tour was completed, they began to fill out the listing papers. Nina had chosen the most awkward place to complete the task—the living room sofa. Papers and pens kept slipping into the crevices of the sofa. Ingrid had suggested they use the kitchen table, but no, Nina thought the living room was more congenial.

After a good deal of discussion and looking at a list of comparable sales, Nina decided on a price. The price was improbable. She wanted to regain all of the money she had spent on the remodel, the original purchase price, and the projected cost of the sale.

"Nina, the market has shifted."

Nina gave the conventional response, "You can always go down, but you can't go up." How many times had Ingrid heard this reply? It was always useless to argue further. So an unrealistic price was set, and the job of selling Nina's house took on a metaphysical dimension.

Three months passed, not one buyer came to look. Nina couldn't wait any longer. Her money was running low. She had given a young man $20,000 to finish the remodel in hopes of increasing the property's chance to sell. He moved in with her, did a few minor changes, and then took off. She reasoned her only recourse was to move to Ethiopia sooner than later.

Ingrid drove to Hornbrook to see Nina off. Nina had packed everything that mattered to her into a Subaru station wagon—seven ferrets plus cages, four dogs, six cats plus cages, a couple of small suitcases. The rest she left behind.

"Ingrid, take down the For Sale sign when I'm gone in case someone suspects the house is vacant."

"Nina, everyone in town knows you are leaving. Why don't we keep the sign up? Statistics show that for sale signs are still one of the best advertising tools in real estate."

"That may be, but let's not have a sign. Email me when an offer comes in. I think my email is *celebrateathousandtimes@mindset.com* or something like that. I'll send you a message when I get set up."

Typical! "Nina, take good care! If you need anything, please let me know."

"Not to worry. I've been there before and still know some people. And I know for sure they don't use pesticides."

"Right! Sure you don't want to sign a price change before you leave? You have to be a little more competitive in this market."

"Ingrid, we've discussed this before. I need a certain amount out of the house in order to live comfortably, even in Ethiopia."

"Life is expensive," replied Ingrid even-handedly.

The two shook hands. Nina climbed into her car and very slowly drove off. *Is she having second thoughts about this venture?* No, the car just seemed to be having a little difficulty gearing up to the task.

Ingrid sympathized with the poor creatures packed into crates on their way to the San Francisco International Airport. *How many hours would they be locked up and how many tranquilizers would they be given for this improbable journey? Would they be injured during the flight?* Ingrid imagined their fear.

When Nina disappeared from view, Ingrid went back into the house to check on doors, lights, etc. Food had been left in the refrigerator—a neighbor would empty and clean it. Slowly she made her way from room to room. The house looked as though Nina was going to return within the hour. *Was this done to fool a would-be burglar?* Ingrid almost believed Nina capable of such rationalization.

This was the first time Ingrid had a chance to thoroughly investigate without fear of scurrying animals or Nina following behind. In the larger bedroom, she found a huge framed photo of Nina, totally nude, lying on a bed with a plucked chicken draped across her stomach. The angle of the picture suggested Nina had photographed herself. She took it off the wall and hid it at the far end of Nina's closet. No use having another distraction when so many already existed.

She went through the rest of the house carefully examining the pictures on the walls in case another portrait of Nina or anyone else needed to be removed, none appeared. Satisfied, she locked the front door and drove home.

No "alpenglow" today, only dust devils in the freshly plowed fields.

Weeks passed before Ingrid received the promised email. All was well except two ferrets died while in detention at the airport in Addis Ababa, the other animals were fine. Ingrid had been told by Nina's neighbor in Hornbrook it cost almost $18,000 to ship the menagerie. *Nina could have continued living in her house for quite a while longer, maybe even long enough to sell it.*

Their correspondence was sporadic. An occasional email asking about the property and house prices in Hornbrook would arrive. Words or letters were omitted, giving the impression of distraction and hurry. The one constant, she was not reducing the price of the house!

Nina's plan was to establish a women's clothing cooperative, similar to the one she had been involved in during her Peace Corps stay in Ethiopia some thirty years earlier. She would recruit Ethiopians to design, cut, and sew dresses from the huge bolts of cloth she had shipped from the States. These dresses would be sold both in Ethiopia and abroad through contacts she had maintained. The demographic group she wanted to target was the older, middle-class Ethiopian woman. Women who were more or less her own age and size. She would branch out to other sizes when the business became successful.

"Ingrid, what do you think?" Nina asked in one of the occasional rambling emails. "You're in business, would you consider this practical?"

Now you ask. The whole trip, this project—all of it is impractical. Come back! Take care of your house! That's what's practical. But Ingrid could not say that.

Ingrid never knew if Nina and her women friends sold any of the garments or if they even made any. Most likely the project never got off the ground. Nina never mentioned it again.

Soon after her arrival in Addis Ababa, Nina began having severe headaches. At first they lasted just a few hours, but then became more severe and more frequent. Nina had been a medical textbook editor and would often self-diagnose. Her symptoms frightened her. The local doctor advised her to fly back to the U.S. for further consultation.

Ingrid did not know how to proceed. Should she contact Nina or should she wait for an email? An email did come. This time it was a mass email Nina sent to all of her friends and acquaintances. "Hello dear ones—an odd turn of phrase, but I mean it! I'm exhausted right now—guess the adrenaline from the surgery's wearing off. Been a little shaky emotionally, but all's well. I've got 6"–7" close set row of staples curving from the top of my head down to behind my left ear. I think it looks like a zipper in my head. Kinder interpretations have been that it looks like a barrette. With more energy, I'd have decorated it with iridescent sequins and ice-blue crystals. The staples come out Tues. Tonight and last night I've gotten up because I cdn't sleep, and I loved getting your e-mails. Today I slept till 2:40 pm. I'll probably be round to a more normal schedule in a few days."

I should have emailed her, darn.

"Been working a little on the ferret-area design for my house in Addis Ababa—yet again constructing an outdoor/indoor setting for them—old energy starting to stir up for projects and fun. Meanwhile Phil and I hve been lying low, going to dinner, watching TV, and generally enjoying life.

What an adventure this continues to be."

Nina had returned to the U.S., had her tumor removed, and taken up with an old boyfriend. The boyfriend was a very brief interlude, but long enough for her to recuperate and plan her trip back to Ethiopia.

Before heading back, she stopped in Hornbrook to rent out her house, take it off the market, and pick up a few items. She stopped at Ingrid's office on her way to San Francisco, but seeing that there were clients in the office, left a note and disappeared.

Why hadn't she waited? I wanted to know how she was feeling. Who are these tenants?

Months again passed before the next email. This time the tone seemed somber and searching.

"Hi—here's something I wrote to another friend. I'm looking for new music in a particular vein, as you'll see, maybe you'll have suggestions. And/or maybe this idea/list will be useful to you.

"Here's the list. These are meant to be 'despair antidotes'—mood lifting and/or calming and/or cheering (w/o, of course, being silly or jarring). Which best matches the bill? Any cuts? Any recommendations? Other genres?

"Mozart-*Concerto for Flute and Harp*

"Teleman-Flute concerti, *Concerto for Three Violins and Orchestra*

"James Galway (soloist)-*The Magic Flute, Annie's Song*

"Debussy-*Claire de Lune*

"Mendelssohn-*Midsummer Night's Dream*

"Chopin-*Polonaises*

"Tchaikovsky-*Waltzes from Sleeping Beauty, Swan Lake,* the *Nutcracker Suite*

"I'd also like some book titles on music—fiction, non-fiction—that talk about how great music is for the mind, body and soul. When I get back to the US, I'll get them frm libraries. Bought a sax for $800. Thinking about Phil and can't seem to focus on it."

Ingrid had no idea what to recommend to Nina. She rarely listened to classical music and never read any books on the power of music to cure a wounded spirit or troubled mind. She never answered the email.

Why did she go back to Ethiopia? Wouldn't it have been better to stay in the U.S. and face all of her demons here?

Ingrid felt ashamed she had not answered Nina's last email. Perhaps she could have reassured Nina this portion of her life was valuable, that middle-age was just another period of discovery that could be satisfying. Ingrid, however, would not allow herself to intrude into Nina's emotions.

One Monday morning, after opening her computer, she saw a message from Nina. "Hello Ingrid—I think of you regularly—it seems as tho we hd a fair amount in common and a lot to share w/each other. So I do send you accounts of life here frm time to time! How are you doing?

"I'm here for the duration fr two reasons—I have friends and an interesting life here, ad I can afford to live reasonably comfortable. I'll ask some friends in Hornbrook to send you a DVD that hz a zillion px of my life here—they are several months old, but the only thing that hs really changed is the way I look. I've lost 40 lbs since you last saw me! Also I hve aged a fair amount ... but never mind!

"My house is still rented, but I have my doubts how the renters are working out. They hd major plumbing problems in the spring—they didn't drain the outdoor pipes before winter—using the rent money to pay the plumber instead of me. Fair enough, I did not have cash to pay the plumber, but months and money hve gone by—still not rent. So far, the bank is being tolerant (I called them a couple of months ago), but that can't go on forever."

The content of this email surprised Ingrid. Nina had always addressed her in the most perfunctory manner, implying a superiority of thought and experience. Now she acknowledged a similarity between them. *Just goes to show how little people understand each other.*

Nina was correct. The bank did not let the nonpayment of the mortgage go on forever. Although Ingrid no longer had a contractual obligation to Nina, she decided to drive the twenty miles to Hornbrook and introduce herself to the tenants. Her appearance might cause concern and rent payments would be forthcoming.

A THUNDEROUS SOUND of barking dogs greeted her as she approached the driveway. *Oh, my gosh, what is going on here?*

A woman approached her as she got out of the car. "Hi, I'm a friend of Nina's. I'm a realtor. I had the property listed for sale. Nina told me about the plumbing problems. Did all that get fixed? By the way, I'm Ingrid Fromm." Ingrid extended her hand to the wary-looking woman.

"Nice to meet ya—I'm Ruth Eastman. Mary, that's my mom, and me rent the place. The water's fine now."

"Nina told me you had dogs. She just didn't tell me how many."

"We rescue dogs—try to find good homes for 'em. Right now, betcha, we got near twenty-five."

"How do you manage to feed all of them?"

"Mom's on Social Security and we get some donations."

"Where do you keep them all?" Ingrid asked with apprehension.

"Got kennels for some of 'em and some of 'em stay inside."

Oh my, gosh! What does the house look like now? Could Nina even begin to sell it at this point?

"Thanks, Ruth. I just wanted to make sure everything was alright. Next time I come, I'll bring some dog food."

The smell of dog feces had drifted into the car. Once out of the driveway, she opened all the windows and took a deep breath. The sun was setting in the west and the eastern hills took on that magical pink and purple that pleased the senses and reminded Ingrid of Alex. She wished her son was riding along, exchanging their mutual appreciation of "alpenglow." Instead her thoughts focused on the house that was to be Nina's sanctuary, but now was the sanctuary for a multitude of dogs.

Maybe the bank's inventory of foreclosed homes was so great this little house would fall through the cracks, not remembered—the dogs and the two caretakers would be spared more hardship. Not likely though!

Her mental energy concerning the house on Cottonwood Creek must have reached Addis Ababa. When Ingrid opened her email at the office, there was a note from Nina. "Great news—a US group called Best Friends will pay the transportation of the vet clinic/lab equipment donated by Dr. Emma Whipple. This means we can set up the vet diagnostic lab—the first one in the country…We are celebrating!!! This will change the vet world in Addis Ababa. Plus it gives me personally something good to participate in and be proud of."

From clothing to veterinary equipment! Oh well, why not?
Nina's focus had begun to shift when an injured and abandoned donkey appeared in her neighborhood. She named
the donkey Edilegna which in Ethiopian means *lucky*. The
donkey had a broken left front knee and two horribly in-
fected hoofs. Everyone, but Nina, suggested euthanasia. She
insisted that Dr. Challa, the local vet, try everything possible
to help Edilegna. Reluctantly, he prescribed a treatment re-
gime. Nina took the donkey in and administered the daily
doses of antibiotics and pain killers. The donkey, most likely,
she assumed, had a massive parasite infection, so in addition
to the other medicine, gave him doses of Ivermectin as well.

Somewhere between the arrival of the vet-clinic lab
equipment and the arrival of Edilegna, Nina began to feel
sick again. "Two new diagnoses—here's something I wrote
to my sister Nell—Feeling a lot better, oddly enough, given
the fact that I finally got a startling v unpleasant diagnosis of
my problem—2 diagnoses, in fact. New hosp where a new
friend, Susan works—high level administrator. Anyway, this
whole thing hasn't sunk in. Right now I am aggravated more
than anything else. Stage 2 right? This aft didn't seem real
at all."

The diagnoses were typhoid fever and multiple large gall-
bladder polyps. She would have the operation on her gall-
bladder as soon as she had recovered from the typhoid.

Ethiopia had not provided an environmentally-healthy
alternative to the U.S. Quite the opposite. Nina's physical
problems had not abated. Her health had gotten worse.
Cause and effect might be impossible to establish, but still
… Ingrid wondered.

CHAPTER 3

A JEWEL BOX

Zola Poe discovered Hilt, California, when she tried to follow the Applegate Trail into Oregon. She'd read a brief history of Lindsay Applegate and his brothers Jesse and Charles, who blazed this alternative to the original Oregon Trail to establish a safer passage. Instead of forging the mighty Columbia River, where two of the Applegate children drowned, this trail would go over the Siskiyou Mountains in northern California, follow a tributary of the Applegate River, and safely deliver pioneers to their destinations. Although safer from natural catastrophes, three hundred emigrants who followed this alternative route were killed by Indians.

Zola, always intrigued by the alternative, decided her summer adventures would be to travel that portion of the Applegate Trail that had become Interstate 5. On her first journey, she saw the sign advising travelers the Hilt exit was approaching. She wasn't sure, but thought she'd read that the road going through Hilt, California, would continue over the Siskiyous into Oregon and the Applegate River Valley.

While trying to decide whether or not to take this exit, she noticed a jackrabbit sitting near the exit sign. As an omen, this certainly did not compare to the grandiose symbol of an eagle sitting on a cactus with a snake in its mouth that commanded the Aztecs in Mexico to stop their migration and settle in the swamp that was to become Mexico City. However, a rabbit's foot is said to bring good luck. And so, an intuitive moment—an epiphany—took hold of Zola as she exited the freeway. She felt as though she'd discovered her own alternative route.

The road curved as it descended into an enchanting valley, at which one end loomed Mt. Shasta and at the other end the less dramatic, but more welcoming, Mt. Ashland. The road became very narrow as it passed Beehive Lane *(What a charming name!)*, curved to the right, and headed north. It passed an old millpond, the still-occupied three-story building of a stagecoach station, and the enormous barns that had housed teams of horses until the last stagecoach departed from Hilt on December 17, 1887, heading south.

For a short distance, the road followed the now nearly abandoned Southern Pacific railroad line that traversed the valley, heading north over the mountains into Oregon. At one point, the road crossed the tracks and veered a little to the west. Here, Zola was able to stop and park her car. She could see the entire valley from this vantage point—Mt. Shasta to the south, the abandoned barns of the stagecoach house, the millpond that had been and still was part of Fruit Growers Supply Company, some cultivated fields, and the meandering Cottonwood Creek. A few houses scattered here and there, a quaint white church with its traditional pointed spire, and some isolated barns were the only signs the valley was occupied.

There was magic in the air. It was as though she'd been transported into the diorama of her brother's train set, almost fifty years ago. She let the place take hold of her spirit and, unconsciously, stretched out her arms as though she could embrace the scene. She must have looked peculiar standing there, her arms encircling nothing, to the driver of the pickup truck who had stopped in front of her.

"Is everything okay? I saw you go by my place a while ago. In this valley you pay attention to the comings and goings of strangers."

"Yes, I am perfectly fine. What a beautiful place this is. Does the valley have a name?"

"Colestin."

Zola folded her hands across her chest as she exhaled the word, "Colestin."

"Well, I have to get going, but if you follow this road, it'll take you past the Buddhist monastery and into Oregon," he said evenhandedly enough, though his look told Zola that he was inviting her to drive on.

She lingered a bit longer and then decided to follow the local's advice and drive onward to Oregon. About two miles up the road, before reaching the California/Oregon state line, she saw a number of prayer flags fluttering from an archway leading to, according to a modest sign, the Buddhist temple. She greatly admired the current Dalai Lama and hoped to meet him either in the States or in a free and sovereign Tibet, once the Chinese saw the error of their ways. She was tempted to drive through the gate to locate the temple. *Next trip I'll plan to spend the whole day scouting this beautiful place. Right now I better head home before it gets dark.*

Zola was excited about this charming valley she'd discovered. Without a doubt, this was the spot where she was destined to be. If she could find the right property, at the right price, she could build the spiritual and holistic retreat she'd always envisioned operating. She could now make use of all those years of therapeutic massage training she'd received in England and apply those principles in a pure and natural setting. Her clients would also receive a thorough diagnosis and printout of their body aura and chakra readings. She'd be able to guide them toward a more fulfilling and meaningful life path based on their physical and spiritual needs. Zola was sure that she'd have a profound effect on all those who came to her Center of Healing. The Dalai Lama would hear of her efforts and reward her with a visit.

The inheritance she'd received from her mother gave her the freedom to pursue her dream. Hilt was clearly the place for such an endeavor. The karma was good. Zola began her search for property. Each weekend for several weeks she drove the thirty miles from her home in Ashland, Oregon, to the Colestin Valley. There were no real estate signs on any of the houses or vacant parcels. Never daunted by the obvious, she went from door to door, asking if property was for sale or if they knew of anyone wanting to sell. Months went by before she was successful in locating a property, a forty-two-acre parcel with an old farmhouse right on Hilt Road next to the stagecoach stop. The house sat on the two-acre parcel near the road. The remaining forty acres were uphill from the house and wrapped around the back of the stagecoach house.

Perfect! She'd live in the old farmhouse while the construction of the Center of Healing took place. The purchase was completed at the end of September, and Zola moved into the farmhouse on a beautiful Indian summer day. The foliage was just beginning to change. The valley was filled with yellow, orange, and red hues, brilliant against the clearest of blue skies and darkest hue of evergreens. She couldn't believe her good fortune.

The forty acres on the hill had a grouping of pine and Douglas fir trees, some oak trees, a meadow, and an old cistern that collected the water coming from a spring originating in Oregon. The water from the cistern then flowed down a pipe into Zola's house. The flow was somewhat irregular—at times very adequate and at other times barely a trickle. Zola couldn't imagine why this might be so. The region was not succumbing to any drought condition. She needed water to develop that parcel, so she began to investigate.

To her dismay, she was told she was not the only property owner who had a right to use the spring; in fact, she only had a quarter share of the water coming from the spring. Her neighbor, the stagecoach house, had a quarter-share, and a property at the end of the valley had the remaining half-share, but in the summer that owner had the right to use as much water as needed for agriculture.

Zola began to correspond with the Oregon Water Board and received documentation indicating that she had not just a quarter-share, but rights to as much water as she needed. The other two shareholders disagreed, and so the "water wars" in the valley began. Several years and court trials later, Zola received an official water certification giving her undisputed rights to as much water as she needed.

The process, however, was costly and arduous. She alienated a number of people by insisting on legal documentation of her rights. Her disagreement with Charlie Wells, her most immediate neighbor and owner of the stagecoach house, was the most acrimonious.

Charlie had been planning to establish an annual asparagus festival in the valley with hundreds of fellow asparagus aficionados coming to the Colestin Valley to view and buy asparagus from his organic fields. He saw the curtailment of his water supply as a deterrent to that plan. He called her a "flatlander"—someone who hadn't been raised in the mountains, someone who had come from "down below," i.e., anywhere south of the Siskiyou County line.

Land and water disputes in the valley had always been settled by a handshake. The securing of the water rights was, however, hugely important to Zola and her plan for the Center of Healing. She did not care what Charlie or the neighbors said. Who was Charlie to talk? After all, he'd only been here ten years himself.

Her next battle was over the shared maintenance of an easement road that would allow her to enter her property from above. She claimed her easement rights did not include a clause stating she was responsible for road maintenance. Her neighbor, Mark Silva, who had his "ranchette" at the end of this road, felt that since he had been maintaining the road with his equipment, Zola should at least pay for some of the gravel necessary for upkeep. Again there were court appearances and decisions, and, once again, the court decided in Zola's favor since no road maintenance agreement had been recorded. Once she won this court case, Mark, who came from a long line of stubborn Portuguese settlers, refused to continue grading the road with his equipment. It became nearly impassable in the winter without a four-wheel drive.

Zola decided to construct a new road into the forty acres. Mark, when he learned of this, tried to block the disputed easement by installing a gate and lock, thus preventing Zola from ever using that entry. Again Zola went to court and again Zola prevailed—the easement road could not be closed to her, but this brought more turmoil into the once tranquil and forgotten valley.

Her greatest battle, however, began when she tried to get permits for various building projects from the county. The zoning for the forty-two acres was designated as secondary farmland which restricted how many buildings could be put on the property and the size of each building. Since the original farmhouse was 1,700 square feet, any other building would have to be 1,200 square feet or less. This required redesigning the original plans for the dome that was the principal structure of the Center of Healing. Another huge problem was getting final approval from the county building department for the overall size of the project since that would require a larger septic system, more leach lines, a sec-

ondary leach field, and on and on. After many, many trips to
planning department hearings, and a number of engineers
later, her designs and layouts were approved.

As the years went by, her resources diminished as did her
spirit. She couldn't understand why every step of the way
was like advancing through a minefield of rules and regula-
tions. Just as she completed one requirement, another was
planted before her.

The battles she'd fought with her neighbors left no room
for an easy truce and had, in fact, undermined the harmony
of the valley. The peace and tranquility she'd felt as a new
arrival had disappeared. The Dalai Lama would now never come. She would not be praised by him, nor would her
Center for Healing become the icon of all healing centers.

She could no longer steel herself against the cold looks of
her neighbors. Every time she drove down the road in her
battered Subaru, she thought they were hiding behind cur-
tained windows waiting for her to pass. She imagined herself
the enemy invader—seen but never greeted, watched but
never spoken to. The silence that she'd welcomed and found
to be healing now became totally untenable. Her hope of
becoming a renowned spiritual guide was shattered. Her
quest for an alternative to the mundane had died.

She rented out the farmhouse, packed her few belong-
ings, headed over the mountains into Oregon, and resettled
in Ashland. Just as the pioneers of long ago, she found that
the alternative path had its own hardships and disappoint-
ments. Her resources had been stretched, and she faced the
inevitable. She called the real estate agent whose name she'd
seen on recently posted sign at the entrance to the valley.

Ingrid Fromm sensed Zola's frustration and weariness after talking with her briefly on the phone while setting up an appointment to meet in Hilt. Zola wanted Ingrid to come out immediately. She wanted to be done with the property as soon as possible. Ingrid explained she needed to do a little research and make a comparative market analysis before the two met so she could advise Zola on setting a price according to recent sales of similar properties. Market conditions for country properties were not particularly good since the price of gasoline had escalated. Buyers were willing to compromise on their preferred locations—better to have a little less privacy and a little more money to buy gas.

The first meeting didn't go well. They'd decided to meet at the State Line. Ingrid assumed this meant where Zola's property merged with the Oregon border off Hilt Road. Ingrid arrived early and waited long enough to realize that she either got the place wrong, the time wrong or both. Disappointed by the "no show," she drove back to her office. As she arrived, one of the agents informed her that "a Zola" was on the phone, and she didn't sound happy.

"If you didn't want my listing, you should've told me. I wasted over two hours driving to the State Line, waiting, and then driving back to Ashland," announced an angry voice.

"I'm very sorry, but I was at the state line," Ingrid countered in her most conciliatory tone.

"How can that be? I arrived quite ahead of time and just sat there twiddling my thumbs. I'll just call someone else."

"I hope you won't do that. Perhaps we could set up a new time and place. I know where your little house is in Hilt. Maybe that would be the place to meet. I would be free Friday afternoon if that's convenient."

"No, we can't meet there. The tenants and I had a little difference of opinion," she replied, without a trace of remorse.

"Well, how about the gasoline station at the top of the hill?" suggested Ingrid hopefully.

"Where do you think I was waiting for you all that time? There, of course, at the State Line."

To Ingrid it sounded as though Zola wanted to finish the sentence with "you idiot," but caught herself in time.

"Zola, I wasn't aware that was the name of the gas station. Again, I am so sorry. Couldn't we meet there on Friday and just start all over again?" Ingrid implored.

"If I had the time to do a little more research on real estate agents, I wouldn't even consider that. My days are full. Call me tomorrow morning, and I will let you know what I've decided."

In real estate there is a saying, "Be grateful for the listings you didn't get." Ingrid hadn't been introduced to that idea yet and quite naively called Zola the next morning to set up another meeting time and place.

Later, reflecting on this first meeting, Ingrid couldn't remember what she'd expected Zola to look like, but it certainly wasn't like the person who appeared before her. Zola was a rail-thin, tiny, wrinkled woman with an old strawhat perched on a skull-like head and a long braid descending from the nape of the neck. Her attire consisted of a longish skirt topped off by a fleece jacket. She wore leggings tucked into nondescript, lace-up boots. There was no sign of breasts or other feminine softness.

Zola's disheveled look brought forth a maternal and sympathetic response in Ingrid. She felt it was now her job to make everything better for this sprite of a woman.

"I hope you brought a decent camera. It's been my experience that photography is a talent few people have. With a good camera, you can at least make a decent attempt."

"Zola, I certainly will try to get some very nice pictures of your property," Ingrid replied professionally.

"I'll take your word for that. Are you able to walk around in those shoes? I want to show you everything so that you'll have a good understanding of how special this property is."

Ingrid ignored the comment about the shoes. "Zola, I pulled a plat map of the forty-two acres—you can point things out as we walk along."

"That won't do. I brought along a diagram of my plan for the Center of Healing and various sanctuaries. Here, for example, we're coming to an ancient pine forest. See how magnificent these trees are!"

Ingrid wasn't sure of the exact definition of a forest, but to her it appeared to be just a large clump of pine and fir trees.

Next, Zola pointed to some oak trees. "Ingrid, be sure to point out this lovely oak grove. In the summer, these oaks provide a habitat for innumerable birds and other wild animals."

"Absolutely!"

And so it went, Ingrid trying hard to see with Zola's eyes the remarkableness of these forty-two acres. It wasn't until they were almost in front of the large dome that something remarkable took hold of Ingrid. Here was a truly amazing structure in this wilderness called Hilt, a building perfectly proportioned and splendid, oriented to the south and Mt. Shasta. It didn't matter the siding was not yet complete or there were no steps, only some wood planks for an entry. The dome, like a lovely jewel box, projected the entirety of Zola's vision for the Center of Healing. Ingrid was now able to grasp this tiny woman's disappointment in the failed dream.

"I constructed the building on this spot because there are six ley lines that intersect. There are more ley lines crossing here than at Stonehenge which only has four. I planned to put the massage table right in the center of the main room so that lines would exercise their spiritual and mystical powers as I massaged my clients. Come, sit down in this chair! It is the exact center of the building where the ley lines converge."

Ingrid did as she was instructed and sat down in an old plastic lawn chair.

"Now, say your name out loud."

Feeling somewhat silly, she quietly said, "Ingrid Fromm."

"No, you need to say it much louder than that," Zola commanded.

"Ingrid Fromm," she shouted, and as she did so, she could hear her own voice echoing inside her head. It wasn't exactly an echo as much as a reverberation of sound passing through her body.

"Did you feel that? That's the ley lines in action." Zola's child-like body was almost dancing with joy. "I want to show you a few more amenities of this property, and then you can take pictures."

They left the Center of Healing and proceeded toward a much smaller dome. "This building was to be for the Dalai Lama. Now, of course, it can be anything."

Did she really believe that the Dalai Lama would journey to

Hilt, California? Amazing! Well, maybe not so amazing. After all, there is a Buddhist temple down the road.

"The only thing left to see is the farmhouse by the road, but I couldn't get in contact with the tenants so you'll have to call them and make an appointment to go through the house. And before you put any pictures and descriptions on the multiple listing, send everything to me first for my approval."

"Of course," replied Ingrid dutifully. *Shoot, what did I get myself into?*

And so the process began—a list price suggested by Ingrid, countered and set by Zola; pictures taken by Ingrid, but selected by Zola; descriptions written by Ingrid and edited or discarded by Zola. Ingrid understood how traumatic this sale was for Zola, and as long as it didn't hinder a possible sale, she let her have her input. On Zola's suggestion, Ingrid designed a brochure highlighting all of the property's salient features and had it professionally printed. Zola gave her a list of all the real estate offices in Southern Oregon that should receive these brochures, either hand-delivered or by mail. Again, Ingrid did not object, mailed most of them and hand-delivered a few.

Weeks went by, but no one called to view the property. Zola became anxious. Was Ingrid advertising enough? Had she made other realtors in the area aware of the uniqueness of this property and location? Ingrid tried to explain to Zola that because the building and infrastructure were not complete, it was difficult to find a buyer who thought the price was reasonable—"No, it isn't the price," Zola said. Ingrid just had to work harder to get buyers there. Once there, they would see the merit of the place.

The summer and fall selling season came and went. Only one showing had taken place, and this had been organized by Zola. One look at the group told Ingrid that these buyers, who had Zola's disheveled appearance, didn't have the means for such a purchase. *Oh well, another afternoon hike.*

LATE ONE WINTER evening, Ingrid was awakened by a phone call. The caller said he had seen a light in the second story of the farm house. He was concerned because he knew the tenants had moved out long ago and the light should not be on. Also, he wasn't sure, but it looked like there were two open windows upstairs. It was snowing heavily in the valley, with substantial wind gusts. Ingrid thanked him and headed back to bed. In the morning she would check on the situation. But she couldn't sleep. She got up, got dressed and began the thirty-minute drive to Hilt. After all, this was one of the reasons for having a heavy-duty four-wheel drive vehicle.

At the Hilt exit, the snow became more serious and the road more slippery. By the time she arrived at the farmhouse, several inches of snow covered the ground. There was no light on upstairs. She went in and checked the windows. All were closed. Had the call been a prank? *When the listing expires, I will not relist this property … I will not relist this property*—was her mantra all the way home.

Winter eased into spring, still no offer on Zola's property. Ingrid tried convincing Zola a price reduction was necessary only to be met with same resistance as always—the uniqueness of the land, the desirability of the location.

"Ingrid, phone for you," called a colleague from across the room.

"This is Ingrid Fromm. How can I help you?"

"Hello. My name is Ambrosio Seth. My friend Brett told me about a property you have for sale in the Colestin Valley. She thought I should take a look at it."

"I am happy to show it to you. When would you like to see it?"

"I'll be at the temple next Thursday. Could I meet you in the afternoon at about two o'clock?"

"Yes, we could meet in front of the farmhouse on Hilt Road."

"Sure, that'll be good. If you have any well reports, maps, or other information about the property, be sure to bring them along."

"Looking forward to seeing you then—thanks for calling."

Finally, this sounds like a "real" buyer!

THE WEATHER WAS absolutely perfect on Thursday. Mt. Shasta showed at its best, still sporting a heavy blanket of snow. The trees had fresh crowns of tender green leaves, and Cottonwood Creek was running high. Ambrosio Seth drove up at exactly 2:00 p.m.

"Mr. Seth, so nice to meet you."

"Call me Ambrosio. Some people even call me Baba-Rum Raisin."

Oh no—but then I shouldn't judge too harshly. Aside from the long ponytail, Hawaiian shirt, and Birkenstock sandals, he looks okay.

"And you can call me Ingrid, of course. Let's start here and then work our way to the rest of the property"

Ingrid had brought maps, reports, and the diagram Zola had provided of her hopes for the property. Ambrosio walked along asking a few questions about this and that, looked at the reports, made some notations on a pad, and seemed altogether engrossed. Ingrid took him inside the dome, asked him to sit in the plastic lawn chair and say his name, just as Zola had instructed her to do. Ambrosio, however, seemed unimpressed by the ley line phenomenon. After about an hour and a half of touring the acreage, Ambrosio thought he'd seen enough. They headed back to the farmhouse to say their good-byes.

"Ingrid, you said something about spring water rights from Oregon. Could you get me those documents?"

"Yes. Give me your fax number and I'll fax them to you. Could you tell me if the property is something you might consider?"

"Well, I consider lots of things. Let me meditate on this. I'm not sure about the karma of the dome. I have a spiritualist friend who is better at sensing the essence of a place. I'd like to bring him to the dome next time I come. Would that be okay?"

"Yes. I can't see the harm in that."

"Good. I'll call you a day or two before I come up the next time. Wishing you much bliss until then."

Bliss, karma, spiritualist, essence—this man is not going to buy anything.

But Ambrosio did buy the property. His friend, the spiritualist, an ordinary-looking fellow, recommended a cleansing ceremony for the dome to expel bad karma. Once Ingrid knew what this exorcism consisted of, she made sure she was present during the burning of sage bundles, fearing the possibility of fire. Other than this somewhat unorthodox procedure, the other investigations of the property were quite normal—water test, septic and pest inspections for the farmhouse, and verification of spring water rights.

The wrinkle came when he tried to get a bank loan. The appraiser had cited the dome structure as a second dwelling. Banks don't like to lend on domes. Now what? Ambrosio inquired if Zola would reduce her purchase price and agree to carry a note for five years with a substantial down payment. Zola's first reaction was a deep sense of outrage. How could the buyer take advantage like that? But the alternative was grim. Seller financing papers were drawn. Zola refused to make another trip down to Hilt to sign additional papers. She was finished, she had done her part. Ingrid, to expedite the closing of the escrow, agreed to hand-deliver the papers to Zola.

Zola's house in Ashland was built against a hillside. The overgrown gardens set the tone of what was going on inside. Items of furniture were stacked on top of each other, papers had been piled up, all seemed in disarray. Zola explained that one of the bathroom pipes had broken the week before and she had to move things around to let the floors dry out before new carpets and vinyl could be installed. This seemed like a reasonable explanation.

Ingrid was instructed to sit down while she, Zola, finished her lunch. From what Ingrid could see, lunch consisted of lettuce leaves and saltine crackers. *Was Zola eating this because she had no money or because she thought this was a healthy lunch?* Ingrid got the papers signed and rushed out.

The lunch scene had greatly disturbed her, but she would not allow herself to think about this sale any longer. She put *Café Cubano* in the CD player and turned up the volume. She played the same CD several times during her drive back to the office. The sunny, lively Latin rhythms distracted her—*what would it take to become a real estate agent in Cuba or Colombia or any Spanish-speaking country? No more Zola, no more Ambrosio, ley lines, water rights, or any other issues connected with the property in Hilt.*

SHE HEARD THE phone ring as she entered the office. "Ingrid, the phone's for you. Do you want me to take a message?"

"No, that's okay. I'll take it," she replied to the floor agent.

"Ingrid, this is Ambrosio. Do you remember Baba Rum-Raisin? You sold me Zola's place a couple of years ago."

Why did I pick up the phone? "Of course, I remember. How's everything going in Hilt? Have you completed the dome and the rest of the work?"

"Not exactly. I did put on some more of the siding and got some of the trenches covered. I worked mostly on the farmhouse, put a new roof on the place, and painted it inside and out. I certainly have increased the value substantially. I was wondering if you'd come out and take a look. I'm thinking of putting the property back on the market."

I will not take this listing. I will not take this listing. I will not take this listing.

"Ingrid, are you still there?"

Why don't I say I'm too busy to handle country properties right now? Zola—oops, Ambrosio, will just have to find someone else this time. Hope he hasn't ruined that lovely dome! Zola's perfect jewel box creation. ...

"Yes—sorry, I got distracted."

"Are you interested?"

"Um.... Sure, why not?"

CHAPTER 4

SURE, WHY NOT?

Another rainy day—so many lately! No pedestrians, no cars, everyone seems to be hiding. In this part of the country rain elicits the same behavior that snow does in other parts of the country; it certainly prevents things from happening. No one even owns an umbrella or, if someone does, it never gets used. I can't think of one person who wears galoshes.

And so, Ingrid Fromm's thoughts drifted as she sat at her functional but outdated thirty-year-old desk in her Yreka, California, real estate office. The entire office had a late '70s style and feel—the Mediterranean look—simulated dark mahogany wood desks and paneling, brown and orange-flecked carpet, rust-colored Moroccan tile at the entry. Computers on each desk were the only visible sign that the twenty-first century had arrived in this frontier region of the state.

While speculating about the habits of her fellow Yrekans, she watched a man cross the office parking lot. He was straight and tall and hatless, no fear of rain evident in his stride. *What fun it would be to walk in the rain with him!* She imagined a version of her younger self—tall, slender and athletic, matching his step, and laughing as she jumped over rain puddles. In fact, this man's positive and lithe gait brought to mind not only a wishful past self, but also the image of a client she had had a few months before—easygoing, confident and absolutely charming.

The client, a youngish man perhaps in his late thirties, was employed by a five-star lodge in the wilds of Alaska as a hunting and fishing guide. Since meals and lodging came with the job, he had saved most of his regular pay along with generous tips he received from the sportsmen staying at the lodge. His plan was to invest this money in real estate, hoping that there would be a greater return than what the banks were offering. Northern California was the location of choice for this investment. He was familiar with Siskiyou County, having spent his summers as a teenager on his grandparents' ranch haying and helping out as an additional ranch hand.

Ingrid remembered that the transaction had been a simple and easy sale between a willing buyer and a willing seller. To top it off, it had been a cash deal without the onerous involvement of a lending institution. It couldn't have been better.

The man walking in the rain, the random thoughts about her Alaskan fishing guide, and her past self, cheered and warmed her like a glass of good red wine or a nap on a quiet Sunday afternoon. The phones were silent. She allowed herself the luxury of reflection.

Company policy stated female agents could not meet an unknown male client alone for the first time unless this meeting took place at the home office. A new client was asked to come to the office first or, if impractical, another agent was to accompany the female agent on the first meeting. To the best of her knowledge, this policy was enacted when a young female agent had been accosted in the field. No one really knew whether the assailant had ever declared himself to be a client, but as with many rules, the "better safe than sorry" thinking prevailed.

Ingrid could still hear the Alaskan's clear, even-toned voice on the phone. His voice had given her confidence the rule could be broken this time without serious consequences. Besides, who would harm a solid, robust woman with a crown of short, permed gray hair? Certainly not a middle-aged man. He'd most likely be looking for a young attractive woman with long flowing blond hair—not another middle-aged ex-wife like Ingrid. And a younger man would surely forgo making advances when confronted with her unadorned, moon-like face. As for danger coming from someone older than herself, that was also highly unlikely. If nothing else, her daily swim routine and exercise sessions had so developed her endurance that she felt she could outrun, if not outmaneuver, any older male. Furthermore, she reasoned, any male predator would most likely be in weak condition—equating the predator's moral and physical decline.

He had called about a little green house advertised in the south county real estate guide. The photo showed a charming house surrounded by huge pine trees. The trees caught his fancy. He wondered where the house was located and if he might be able to look the next day around 9:00 a.m. The house was in Weed, a town some twenty-five miles south of Yreka. Did he know where that was? Sure, he knew. His grandparents' ranch was just a little east of there. In fact, he would be coming directly from an early morning pheasant hunt on the ranch.

She recalled feeling uneasy. Hunting meant guns. He would most likely have a gun or two in his pickup. Her mind conjured up the image of the young local men with pickups and guns strapped to racks on the rear window and menacing dogs in the bed of the truck. Her confidence had waned—not because of fear of physical harm—it just wasn't the best scenario for making a sale.

A number of months had passed since she closed on the Weed property sale and Ingrid was surprised how easily she remembered the events, his voice, his appearance, and her feelings. She had arrived at approximately 8:50 a.m. at the property in question. She couldn't tolerate tardiness and was always disappointed in those not motivated by the same standard. She wanted the house to be open when he arrived. Fumbling with locks or combinations, she felt, colored the client's confidence in an agent. *There ought to be a course for realtors on how to open front doors with the least amount of stress!* When possible she always wanted the lights turned on for a bright and cheerful welcome.

The house was open and ready to show with the lights on, but he didn't arrive at 9:00 a.m., nor 9:15 a.m., nor 9:30 a.m. Ingrid reminded herself that she should have listened to her first instinct; and the appointment was most likely a waste of time. Real estate buyers are not the most dependable individuals. After an appointment has been set, other activities such as hunting can take precedence with the buyer. Sometimes the buyer would not call to advise the agent of a change in schedule, assuming that the failure to appear was sufficient notice. Ingrid considered "no-shows" as rude and lacking respect for her profession.

She remembered feeling a bit disheartened as she walked around the little house checking if the lights had been turned off and doors secured. Sellers have no sympathy for agents who leave lights on, doors unlocked.

Now where the heck is that front door key? Did I lock the back door? I don't want to drive back to check. While trying to find the front door key in several possible pockets of her purse, she heard the sound of a truck in the driveway. She stepped outside, stood on the porch, and waited with arms folded. He jumped out of the truck with youthful ease. Quickly approaching the porch with exuberant steps, he acknowledged, with an extended hand, "Sorry I'm late." She shook his hand, but had not expressed the expected, "Oh, that's okay." She simply said, "The house is still open, take a look!"

He reminded her of a current well-known soccer player whose picture she had seen advertising men's briefs in a fashion magazine. She recalled her attention had focused a little longer on this ad than usual. And just like the soccer star in the ad, this man exuded vigor and confidence. Both men seemed to know that their bodies would do exactly as they wished them to do—graceful and charming young men with easy and open faces. *If only I would have had their confidence at that age!*

Her disappointment had vanished. Like two friends, they ambled from one brightly painted room to the next. The children must have been consulted when the colors were cho-

sen—lilac walls and a wispy-blue cloud ceiling in the first
bedroom, metallic blue with Spiderman suspended from the
ceiling in the next bedroom, dark moss green with white
trim in the master. The rest of the rooms had been spared
the creative touch. The kitchen was *de rigueur* white as was
the bathroom, and the living room walls were dirty gray or
dirty brown—she couldn't remember.

He had listened good-naturedly to her description and
explanations. He didn't as much follow her through the
house as walk with her, sometimes tilting his head toward
her to hear more clearly what she had to say. *What was the
feeling I had then—a lightness of being?*

When they went outside she alluded to the possibility
of a problem with the septic system. At this point he lost
interest and mentioned that his friends were probably still
waiting for him at the ranch, he wasn't too sure about the
property. She told him about another house with a nice
fenced yard and lots of potential. The house needed a little
work, but was livable and cozy. There was also an 18 x 20-
foot detached garage.

"Would you be available to view the property tomorrow?" And, in her most cajoling tone, "Would 10:00 a.m.
be better?" He didn't answer immediately, as if pondering
several possibilities. "Sure, why not?"

Sure, why not? Had she ever responded so indifferently to a
sincere offer? Of course she had—probably many times without realizing a friend or acquaintance had hoped for a more
heartfelt response. If the emotions between people were in
harmony while conversing, there would be fewer difficulties
or misunderstandings. They wouldn't have to agree on the
content of their discussions, just on the emotion.

"Sure, why not?" Wasn't that what she had said so off-handedly to Mr. Bendenelli? Ingrid recalled her first meeting with him on the slopes of Mt. Hood while instructing a high school boys ski team on the correct up and down motion when changing direction on skis. She was working her first job out of college teaching at a parochial school for boys and assigned the ski team as her extra-curricular teaching duty. While she knew how to ski, her technique was questionable.

It had been one of those stormy afternoons—almost white-out conditions—that were frequent in the Cascades that year. The boys were anxious to finish the up and down drill and return to the coziness of Timberline Lodge, the only warm spot on the mountain, and finish their leftover lunch.

Mr. Bendenelli was a member of the Mt. Hood volunteer ski patrol unit. She remembered thinking him to be old, but maybe he hadn't been so old after all. On one of his patrol runs, he had paused to watch her attempts at instructing the boys. It must have been apparent that she was struggling. Not only was she lacking in skill and knowledge, she was not in command of the situation. The teenagers were pushing and shoving each other, exaggerating the demonstration. Had she been a little more confident her youth might not have hindered her so much.

After watching her demonstrate the art of changing edges, Mr. Bendenelli had offered his help. Wasn't it part of his job to make sure everyone could safely maneuver down the slopes?

"Sure, why not?" had been her offhanded response.

From then on he would find them every Friday afternoon

on the slopes. Nothing was ever pre-arranged. He would ski up to the group, wave to the boys, extend his gloved hand to shake her gloved hand, linger just a while, then turn and ask the boys, "What do you want to work on this week?" After a short explanation of a technique, he would enthusiastically shout, "Ingrid, let's you and me show them how it's really done." Then again shouted with the same good cheer at the end of a session, "Ingrid, that team of yours is really looking good. Great job!"

"I think it's you, not me," she would reply.

The ski season ended on a positive note, thanks to Mr. Bendenelli. The boys, in fact, won a few medals at the end of the season inter-scholastic ski races. Her "team" had also discovered that she, the only female coach at the high school, did not receive a stipend for coaching. They threatened to lead a school-wide protest. The administration relented and included a "bonus" in her February paycheck.

Ingrid never saw Mr. Bendenelli after that winter, but now wondered why he had looked at her so intently. Had her nonchalant acceptance of his help reminded him of some past "Sure, why not?" reply he had made? Or, was he searching for an emotion she did not yet understand?

For her second showing, she had again arrived early, followed her routine, and then waited for his arrival. This time the truck pulled up the driveway at 10:00 a.m. as scheduled. As before, she noticed how quick and light his movements were. It wasn't that long ago she had been able to move just like that. Her heart ached just a little, not so much for the physical attributes of youth, but the possibilities that youth implied.

He smiled, shook her hand, and followed another guided

tour, gracefully stepping from one room to the next—such easy movements in and out of doorways. He could see some of the good points of the house, but altogether he felt it would take too much time to do the repairs. He was going to leave the area soon for Alaska and wanted to rent out the property before beginning the new season at the lodge.

She had suggested he follow her to the office so she could give him a computerized visual tour of available properties in his price range. This would facilitate and shorten his search time.

During her drive back to the office, she had barely noticed the green hills surrounding the equally green valley floor with black cows scattered in the fields like so many mounds of dirt. This lush pastoral view always pleased her. It was so rare and always brief in the high desert climate of the Shasta Valley—a mirage of sorts that disappeared in a blink of an eye.

Another feeling took hold of her. She felt as though she had had a most delightful waltz with an accomplished partner—floating from room to room, dancing to the tune of casual reflections about the property's shortcomings. The comments were made lightly, without censor or judgment, a dance in three-quarter time.

Most clients expressed their dislike in much more negative tones, almost to the point of hostility. It always made her come to the defense of the maligned property, rightly or wrongly. This time, however, the house had not been demeaned in any way. There had been no reproach implied as they waltzed out and gently closed the door. The house simply did not fit his needs.

At the office, they had talked at length, making casual

comments about the various properties found on the computer search—maybe too large, perhaps too expensive, too
far away. His soft manner never changed. As they talked,
youth and age assimilated into a timeless form, a partner-
ship of sorts.

She had suggested more showings, but that would not be
possible until the following week. He and his girlfriend were
leaving for a few days. He gave her a friendly and direct look
as he shook her hand. Yes, next week would be fine.

A girlfriend, of course! What was she like—young, pretty? They probably were well suited—for the moment.

The slight pressure of his hand lingered. In her twenty
plus years as a realtor, she had shaken many hands, embraced
many shoulders, and never thought to reflect on feelings of
gratitude or friendship those short physical contacts con-
tained. When a client liked to hug, she allowed herself to be
hugged—all appropriate and professional. Yet now, she felt
a surprising significance to this universal acknowledgement.

A deal was consummated shortly after his return. He had
decided on a well-cared-for manufactured home at the edge
of town with city utilities and an oversized lot. The property
would be easy to rent and not too much for him to worry
about while in Alaska.

The house inspections had been made and reports issued.
There was a final walk-through prior to close of escrow. All
findings of the property's condition were reviewed once
more. He stood close to her as she pointed out some of the
misgivings she had. He acknowledged her concerns with a
nod and a look of appreciation. She was looking out for
him. His manner suggested Ingrid had done a great job for
him and that he had consequently found the ideal property.

She had mentioned that unless he had any questions about the property, her part in the transaction was complete. She thanked him for his business, gave a generous gift certificate for the local fly-fishing shop, and wished him success. They shook hands. She couldn't remember who withdrew first.

As usual, she had reviewed all the forms before handing her broker the transaction file. She came across one form where his initials were missing. Afraid that he might already have left for Alaska, she called him to see if he could stop by to initial the document. She explained that her broker was demanding in that way—the files had to be complete or he would hold up her commission check. He agreed to do it the next day, though not as cheerfully as she had hoped.

HE FRAMED THE doorway of the entry—incredibly perfect and complete—the most complete and perfectly proportioned person she thought she had ever seen. He came into her office. He was glad she had called because he wanted to contact the previous owner concerning the water shut-off valve for the sprinkler system. She made the contact within minutes. Problem solved! He initialed the overlooked document and wondered how she could have caught such a small omission.

The same parting as before—he stood up and with his usual direct and inclusive look, extended his hand—palm-side up. She slid her hand in his without rising. A warm ephemeral connection happened for her. Had Mr. Bendenelli felt such a connection with her through those cold, thick ski gloves the last time they shook hands? She hoped he had.

CHAPTER 5

THE RAIN MELTED IT

"Who's on the floor?"

"I am," answered Ingrid.

"It's an up-call. Some guy wants to be picked up to look at a house in Yreka."

Just my luck. Picked up, huh? Probably lives at the other end of the county. No car and no money, the two seem to go together. If it's over ten miles from the office, I will not go. I'll just say, no! Absolutely not!

"Hi, this is Ingrid Fromm. How can I help you?"

She heard some shuffling and giggling in the background before this pleasant and polite voice announced. "I'm George Taylor. Saw your ad in the paper—cheap homes in Yreka. Where are they? How much are they?"

Sounds like a bunch of kids in the background. Could be a prank call.

"Mr. Taylor where do you live? And where are you calling from?"

"Call me George, everyone does."

"Thanks, George. And you can call me Ingrid. You said you needed to be picked up."

"I'm in Montague –Mrs. Krammer's place.

Didn't I just read something about that in the Daily News? *At least it's close by.*

"George, have you talked to a lender about getting a loan?"

"Nope. I won't need a loan unless I buy a really big place, but I don't need a really big place, so I won't need a loan."

"So, this will be a cash transaction?"

"A transaction? I just want to buy a place to live."

"That's what I meant to say. You want to buy a house with the cash you have, right?"

"Right! Then I don't have to follow any rules, but my own."

I knew it. That polite voice is just a cover-up.

"Can someone bring you to my office tomorrow? Before we go look at different places, we need to discuss all types of options you might have. I can show you some possibilities on the computer and that way we won't waste time looking at unsuitable listings."

"Does the senior bus stop at your place?"

"I think the senior bus will stop almost anywhere you want it to stop—within reason, of course. George, can you give me your phone number just in case something comes up and I'm not going to be at the office?"

"Krammer said the phone's only for emergencies. Just leave a message."

After she hung up, she realized she forgot to get the phone number. She wondered why he could only use the phone for emergencies. The number would be easy to find.

"Do any of you know anything about a place in Montague called Krammer's?" Ingrid asked the assembled agents.

"Sure. It's an adult care facility for men and women who have a court appointed guardian, owned and operated by Mrs. Krammer."

No car—care facility—would there be a trustee involved? No use worrying about something that may not even happen. He might not show up, he might not have proof of funds. So many possibilities!

But George showed up on the appointed day at the appointed time, cheerful and excited about the possibility of buying a home of his own.

"I'm George," he announced to the group as he entered the office.

Most of the agents looked up and smiled at him. It was the type of smile people reserved for a precocious six-year old who has done or said something charming. And, in response to their smiles, George waved to the assembled group.

He was a somewhat portly, almost middle-aged man with dark hair and a ruddy complexion. As he talked his hands and feet moved—he was like a bouncing ball, here and there and everywhere—a middle-aged Humpty Dumpty on the verge of falling.

"George, I'm Ingrid. Come on over to my desk where we can discuss the type of place you have in mind to buy."

George was happy to talk about his dream, his finances,

and his current living situation, which was not to his liking at all. Ingrid found out how much money he had to spend, how he acquired this money and, most importantly, how she might verify the accuracy of this information.

After twenty years as a real estate agent, she had become wary of clients who said they had the means to buy property, when in fact the money was some illusory settlement that never came or, when it did come, was not enough to afford the properties that she had spent days showing.

It appeared that George's father left him a nice sum of money with only a rudimentary bank guardianship. He only needed to show how he was to spend the money and explain the reason why, and the bank would review the request and, if it deemed it to be reasonable, would allow him to withdraw the money.

Ingrid was able to show him several properties on the computer that might fit his pocketbook and desire to become independent. After much discussing and relooking at the listed properties on the computer, they decided that Ingrid would pick him up the following day at Mrs. Krammer's and show him the selected properties in Yreka.

Montague, a small, very rural town with a population of less than two thousand, was only six miles east of Yreka, the county seat. This met Ingrid's ten-mile pick-up distance. George was waiting in front of Mrs. Krammer's when Ingrid arrived at the settled upon time. With him was his roommate and good friend Darryl. Darryl was a little younger than George, but appeared to have the same happy aspect. *Maybe Mrs. Krammer gave all of her residents orange juice with a happy-go-lucky additive in the morning.* The two settled into the back seat of her Jeep. They joked and laughed like adolescents all the way into Yreka. Ingrid thought she heard one of them say, "Drive on!"

The first stop was in a manufactured home park close to the Interstate 5 exit within walking distance of a few convenience stores, a service station, and two Mexican restaurants. Quite a change from Montague!

Ingrid sensed George's excitement. As the county seat, Yreka is the largest town in Siskyou County, with almost 7,500 inhabitants. There would be more things to do—bowling, concerts in the park during the summer, shopping at Walmart, and lots of restaurants. Yreka even has traffic lights—three on Main Street, to be specific.

All of this implied activity to George and an escape from the boredom he now felt. He wouldn't even need a car or the senior bus. He could walk to the store to get his groceries. He could walk to the park and to the community theater.

The mobile home was only two years old. The appliances had hardly been used. The carpet was spotless. In addition, it had both central heat and air, something George really wanted. There were two bedrooms and two bathrooms, a comfortable living area open to a kitchen, and a utility room with washer and dryer. The landscaping was minimal, some bushes set among decorative bark. This was perfect. He didn't need to look any further. This was the house he wanted. The price was right, the location fantastic.

Darryl, who had been relatively silent, remarked, "Man, we can have some great parties here."

George decided he shouldn't wait to make an offer. Someone else might make an offer on the property and he would miss out. He clapped his hands in joy and bounced around the mobile. *He certainly has no inhibitions.*

"George, I'm going back," said Darryl suddenly. "I'll just

start walking. Somebody'll give me a ride."

"Darryl, don't tell Krammer what I'm doing. This'll really surprise the old battle-ax."

Ingrid and George went back to the office to write the offer. The contract needed to be reviewed by the bank before being submitted to the seller. George thought that that would not be a problem. He was sure they would approve the purchase. This way he would not spend the money foolishly.

Ingrid usually spent between forty-five minutes to one hour putting a contract together with a first-time buyer. Terms had to be decided and contract language needed to be explained to the novice buyer. At the end of two hours, George and Ingrid finally reached the last page when George said, "I don't know if I have that much money left in my savings account." *Oh no, here we go again! Why didn't I have him bring me some type of verification of funds before going through all of this?*

"George, sign the last page so we have a finished purchase contract the bank can review. Then call the bank—use my phone. Have them fax over a letter stating you have sufficient funds to buy this house."

"Sure, that way I'll know how much I have to spend."

"Great."

"Could you look up the bank number for me? I *always* talk to the manager. He's in charge of my money."

Ingrid looked up the number, dialed it for George, and handed him the receiver once she heard the ring at the other end.

"Tell Kevin that George wants to ask him something. I need to know how much money I can spend on a house. I'll wait. I've got time."

Sure, he has time. He's just like everyone else. Everyone thinks that the realtor has all the time in the world—she's available whenever it is convenient for them—that she has no life beyond real estate. In this case, that's true, but beside the point.

George seemed to have good rapport with the bank. Within minutes the manager, Kevin, came on the line to tell George how much money he still had. He promised George a letter with this information would be sent to the real estate office before the end of the day. Much relieved, Ingrid shook George's hand and congratulated him on the huge step he was taking.

"Okay, George. We're finished for today. Let me drive you home."

"Thanks. This is going to be so much fun."

I sure hope so.

Days and weeks passed. The normal house buying procedures took place. On the thirtieth day, the property was recorded in his name and Ingrid met him at the park, key in hand.

"George, it's yours. Take good care of it and call me if you have any problems."

"Thanks. Guess what, Darryl's movin' in with me. He promised to pay for some of the bills. And, guess what else! He bought a car. Now I can really have fun."

"I imagine you two are used to each other by now. Thank you very much for your business. I really appreciate it."

The sky was a brilliant blue, all seemed fine with the world as she drove out of the mobile home park. The phrase, "a lightness of being," came to mind. She chided herself for always anticipating the worst. George turned out to be a model customer. The sale had been simple.

The phones were ringing a little more often at the office. Spring was in the air and thoughts turned to new beginnings—i.e., new homes. This was all good. Ingrid was looking forward to new customers. Selling real estate gave her the opportunity to meet all types of personalities and, for a short while, become intensely involved in their lives.

One of her customers observed, at the end of a transaction, "I feel like I should invite you for Thanksgiving dinner. We now know each other so well."

But the best part for me is to have it end before we all know each other any better—I like the graciousness of the superficial. I like the fact we are careful with each other, hesitate a little before making comments, or giving opinions.

She understood the common fears that most people had when making, what is often termed, "the single largest investment in life," and tried to minimize it so that there would be no "buyer's remorse." In most of the cases, she succeeded.

"Ingrid, George is on the phone." Everyone in the office knew who George was and he knew everyone by name as well. His good nature was appreciated by all. He was always a good source for an updated weather report. Whenever he came into the office, someone would ask him, "Hey George, how's the weather going to be the rest of the week?"

"Hi, George, what's up?"

"I want to sell my house."

"George, you've only been there a few months. Why do you want to sell?"

Darryl's girlfriend is shackin' up with him. There's people over all the time. It gets me nervous. They eat my food—

don't clean up the mess. Don't even pay me. Besides, I used to live in Hawaii. I wanna go back. I shouldn't've bought this place. I wanna sell."

"Are you absolutely sure you want to sell? Don't you want to give it more time? If you and Darryl don't get along, why don't you just ask him and his girlfriend to move out? Give it a few more months, maybe it will get better."

"No, I really wanna go to Hawaii."

"All right! I'll come over tomorrow at about 10:00 a.m. and get you to sign the listing papers and take new pictures."

"Could you make it about eleven o'clock?" Darryl 'n' Susan don't get up before then."

"Sure, that will be fine. See you then."

I knew that sale had been too easy. How am I going to explain to him he will lose money selling so quickly?

When she got there the next morning, George told her that he had purchased his one-way ticket to Hawaii at the travel agency in town. Darryl and Susan were moving out by the end of the week. Darryl was going back to Mrs. Krammer's and he didn't know and didn't care where Susan was going. He, George, was happy to be leaving the mobile home park. None of the neighbors even talked to him, and several had complained about the noisy parties Darryl had.

"George, how am I going to get in contact with you when we get an offer?"

"I'll call you once I get there and have a phone."

"Well, if you are absolutely, positively sure you want to do this, let's get listing papers started. Before I forget, I'm going to write our toll-free number on the back of my card so you can call when you need to."

"I'm getting low on cash. Hope it sells soon."

"You know that you're not going to make any money selling right now, not when you have to pay real estate commission plus all the other selling costs?"

"I don't care. I can't live here anymore."

And so George left for Hawaii, Honolulu, Oahu. Weeks
passed and he still didn't call to give her a phone number or
address where he might be reached. Ingrid got worried.

How would she contact him there?

When he finally did call, he mentioned how lucky he had
been to make contact with a group of guys who had a house
where he could stay. He gave Ingrid the phone number, but
asked her not to call unless she really needed him.

After this initial contact, George began to call her almost
everyday. Had she found a buyer yet, he was running out of
money? His housemates were going to ask him to leave if he
didn't give them more money. What was the weather like in
Yreka, the weather in Honolulu was great. This became an
almost daily routine.

One morning after such a call from George, Ingrid's broker announced to everyone in the office, "I just talked to
George in Honolulu. I told him he is not to use our business
line to give us any further weather reports. If he wants us to
know what the weather is like, he should use his own money
to call. Ingrid, when he calls again, tell him the same thing
or you can pay for those calls yourself."

To head off more unpleasantness with her broker, Ingrid
decided to call the number George had given her. Whoever
answered the phone had no idea who George was.

Now what? I should have expected something like this. He
probably told everyone he was going to make a huge amount of
money when he sold his home. Someone then hit him over the

head and stole his identity. George might be decaying in some
Honolulu alley. I hope not. Ingrid, stop!

She hoped George was alive and well and was brave
enough to call again so she could ask him about that situation. Several weeks went by, no call from George.

And, as no buyer for his mobile was in sight, she relaxed
and pushed this problem to the back of her mind. She would
worry about it all when there was an offer on the table.

The offer did appear, it was a good offer, not to be tri-
fled with. Now the search would begin in earnest. *Where on*
Oahu could George be found? Ingrid tried the same number
again, and as before, no success. She was tempted to try the
police, but then she couldn't be sure if George's character
could withstand such scrutiny.

"Ingrid, would you take a collect call from Honolulu?"
asked the floor agent.

"Absolutely! George, is that you?"

"One of the guys at the house told me some lady's been
callin'."

"That's strange. Whoever answered my calls always said
that they didn't know who you are."

"Ya, well I'm really not stayin' there. I got a new place."

"Could you give me that number before I forget to take
it down?"

"I'll have to get it to you later—can't remember it now."

"George, I have an offer on your property. It's a good
offer. You might lose a little money because you have to pay
a commission, but not really that much."

"Great. I need money."

"I have to be able to send the offer to you or fax it so that
you can look it over, sign, and send it back. How can I get

it to you?"

"Send it to my new P.O. box. It might get lost if you send it to the house address. You can't trust nobody there."

"I thought you weren't staying there anymore."

"Well, sometimes I do."

What in the world does that mean?

One problem solved. The offer was sent via priority mail that same afternoon.

Within a few days the original envelope came back with an "unable to deliver" sticker attached. The next time George called, she became a little testy with him. Being testy with George didn't produce the desired results. He was adamant that he had told her to send it to the house address, the P.O. box was for emergencies only.

What else could she do but send it out again, this time to the house address. She made sure it wouldn't be too difficult for him. She highlighted in yellow every spot he needed to sign. Additionally, she enclosed a self-addressed stamped envelope for the return mail. This time the signed offer came back, not one signature or initial was missing. *I wonder if George really signed all of that himself. Looks like his signature, but there are good imitators everywhere. The title company will require their forms to be notarized. I refuse to worry over the authenticity of these signatures!*

All went well until George was required to complete the title company's paperwork. The first mailing was lost. The second mailing did not arrive either. For each failed mailing, George was going to have to pay the fifty dollar FedEx charge. The charge was going to be deducted from the net proceeds of the sale. This got his attention or someone's attention because the third mailing was returned quickly, signed and notarized.

One more step and Ingrid would be finished with George. *Hang in there Ingrid. The end is in sight.*

The title company asked her to find out how George wanted to receive his money—could they direct deposit it to his bank account, the safest process, or did he want the check sent to him. He requested that they send him his check. This time he was to make sure to give them the correct address because they were sending it by registered mail.

"Sure, send it to the same address," said George cheerfully. "Ingrid, tell 'm to hurry. I don't have much cash left."

"George, are you okay there? Who are these people you are living with?"

"Just some guys. I'm outta here when I get my money."

The title company let her know when the check was sent out. Ingrid asked to be informed when they were sure that the check had been cashed.

A few days after the title company had sent the check, George called.

"Ingrid, tell 'm to send me another check."

"Didn't you get the check?"

"Yeah, but after I got the check, Tom and me were takin' the check to the bank. We were ridin' our bikes when there was this downpour. Man, if you've never lived in Hawaii, you've got no idea how hard it rains. I had the check in my shirt pocket. The rain melted it."

"That's amazing. I'll be glad to give them a call to see what the procedure is."

For a moment or two she was totally stunned. Had she heard laughter in the background? She couldn't be sure. She called the title company. As far as they knew, the check had been cashed.

Did George cash the check? Was the money stolen from him? Did someone convince him that he could get another payment by telling the story of the melted check?

Ingrid really didn't want to know! And yet, the uncertainty of George's whereabouts and well-being bothered her.

I should have called Honolulu police and had them investigate that address.

The contradiction between George's middle-aged appearance and his childlike character came to mind whenever she thought of him. Although she had conducted the purchase and sale of his property in an ethical and professional manner, there remained a deep regret—had she acted as her brother's keeper?

CHAPTER 6

THE TRAP DOOR

As Ingrid drove leisurely to her next appointment, her thoughts turned to her dream the night before. She often had dreams, but could recall few details upon waking. This dream was different—the colors, sounds, participants, and scene were still vivid. She was walking barefoot on a wind-swept deserted beach, one hand holding her shoes, the other pushing her hair back so she could see ahead. Her compan-ion, a golden retriever, followed her. Occasionally they en-countered small streams that had reached their destination and merged with the incoming tide. These streams were easy to cross. She recalled cold sand squishing between her toes as she walked through shallow water. She and the retriever alternately walked and ran, pushing themselves into the wind. They'd come upon an oddly shaped pool, deep, rectangular with clear shimmering water so crystalline she could detect individual grains of sand at the bottom.

She'd jumped the pool easily and waited for the dog, but he just stood looking at the water. After she called him numerous times, he finally jumped. Instead of leaping across, however, he'd leaped into the air. His ears flapped as he'd plunged into the pool. She watched him glide through the water, weightless. He reached the bottom without as much as a ripple in the water above. She'd been afraid he would drown. To her amazement, the dog stretched out peacefully at the bottom of the pool, appearing perfectly content.

Her dream ended there—strange dream, but then most dreams seem strange when driving in the light of day.

Ingrid loved the drive from Yreka to Dunsmuir along Interstate 5. From the scenic Shasta Valley with the looming beauty of Mt. Shasta to the Sacramento River Canyon, every aspect was familiar and extraordinary. Most of the small towns along the highway could not escape the drone of the freeway. Only Dunsmuir, hidden in the canyon below the freeway, shrouded in a blanket of trees, shrubs, and flowers, and buffeted by splashing sounds of the Sacramento River, had escaped the noise and commerce that came with the twenty-first century.

A railroad company helped start this town, and its trains still blasted up the canyon each day, stopping briefly to pick up and drop off a passenger or two before disappearing into the world beyond. When the clouds hung in the canyon, a sense of solitude hovered over the town. As the departing trains moved faster and faster into the fog, only their eerie, echoing whistle reminded the denizens it had been there— one last blast and then silence, isolation.

Dunsmuir had a forgotten aura, a place no one knew about, and yet, strangely, two of the best restaurants in the county were located in this hamlet of less than two thousand. Fly fishermen, who scour the world for the perfect fishing hole, came on a regular basis to try their skills on the Sacramento River, and they, evidently, like to eat well and often enough to keep the restaurants in business.

Ingrid liked how the early afternoon shadows gave the town a somber and mysterious aspect. She had thought of opening her own real estate office here. She wouldn't make much, but then again, it might satisfy a deeper need for a new lifestyle. When she mentioned this possible move to a colleague, she was surprised at the strong reaction.

"Charming? Are you crazy? That town has bad karma. I make a point of never going there if I can help it. You can't be serious about moving there!"

Her friend couldn't exactly say what the bad karma was.

"It's just spooky there. The sun comes late and leaves early. There's shadows everywhere and I need lots of light. Didn't you hear about the woman who had her feet cut off while she was waiting for the train?"

"Yes, but the woman wasn't exactly waiting for the train. She'd fallen asleep drunk near the tracks and didn't hear the train approach."

"Where else would that have happened, but in Dunsmuir?"

Probably in any place where there is a railroad track.

Nevertheless, she was always pleased when clients called to look at property there. Many houses were built on sloping canyon walls necessitating huge basements to keep the first floors level with the street. These basements were sometimes turned into garages, if possible, or cold storage for vegetables or canned goods. The homes most often had large sun porches to let in all possible light. Before the invention of the dryer, these porches were used to hang laundry in the winter.

No shadows or fog today! The canyon was full of light— green, yellow, orange, red, and every color in-between as she arrived to oversee a home inspection on just such a house. The house had been built for a railroad clerk and his family some eighty years earlier, and not much had changed since then—no central heat or air conditioning, no dishwasher, old single pane wood windows, linoleum in the bedrooms, Douglas fir flooring in the living room, small rooms, small closets, a wood burner in the kitchen, and sweet, flowered curtains around the kitchen sink. There was also an old wringer washing machine on the sun porch, the laundry area, but no dryer.

How could anyone not appreciate the charm of such a place?

Theresa, her customer, had fallen in love with Dunsmuir and also with this house surrounded by a white picket fence, rose bushes in front and a giant apple tree, which seemingly hung on to the steep slope of the backyard by sheer willpower. It reminded her of her grandmother's house she, her siblings, and parents visited almost every Sunday and holiday when she was a child.

"This is it, I know it. I have to have this house. I feel so at home here."

"Theresa, I'm not so sure," said her husband John. "There doesn't seem to be anywhere we can hook up a washer and dryer. Where's the 220?"

"That doesn't matter, the old wringer will do. Besides,

Kenny is a contractor and he can fix that," she assured him.

"Theresa, don't you remember? I told you, when I was a kid watching my mother use her wringer, I got my hand stuck in the rollers. It just about pulled my whole arm out."

"Well you're not a kid anymore!"

No doubt about it, Theresa wanted this house.

Ingrid had never figured out if she should point out the shortcomings of a property. If they are not an obvious health or safety hazard, why not just let her clients' dreams dictate the purchase?

Two sisters had inherited the house when their ninety-five-year-old mother passed away at home the previous year. Since neither of the sisters wanted to move back to Dunsmuir, they instructed the agent to emphasize to any buyer the house, although old, was in perfect condition and being sold in its "as is" condition without any warranties or guarantees.

"Theresa, John," she told them, "I think you should, at minimum, have a home inspection made. Old houses sometimes have hidden problems, and I think it would be best to have it done by a licensed home inspector. I know your son Kenny is a contractor, but should something come to light after you buy the house, I think you'll have better recourse in getting it fixed if a third party professional had done the inspection instead of your son."

To this they agreed, and an inspection was to take place on this fine fall day.

On her way into town, Ingrid stopped at the listing agent's office to pick up the front door key and make sure everyone had been advised of the inspection. She and Anna Perez, the sellers' agent, chatted a bit.

"Be careful! I haven't had a chance to pray over this house. I usually pray over all of my houses. In fact, I've thought I might let the listing on this one go. I just don't have a good feeling."

"Do you really pray over all of the houses you list?" *Who in the world prays over a house in this day and age?*

"Absolutely, you never can tell! I had a strange feeling when I walked through that house. Don't take any chances!"

"Oh, Anna, it's such a beautiful day, no clouds, no fog, no slippery ice-covered streets, just wonderful colors and a blue sky. This is probably the most perfect day I have ever seen in Dunsmuir."

"I know, it is a beautiful and fine day, just be careful in that house."

The buyers, along with their son Kenny and daughter-in-law June, were waiting for her in front of the house. Ralph, the home inspector, had not yet arrived. Ingrid decided to start her agent's visual inspection as required by the California Bureau of Real Estate while waiting for him. Halfway through her inspection, Ralph arrived. They all followed him around a bit, asking questions about the soundness of the house.

"How do I get down to the basement?" Ralph asked.

"Follow me," Ingrid said. "The opening is on the sun porch. It's a trap door that hinges to the wall. I think it'll take two people to open it. At least, it took two of us when I showed it the first time."

Everyone else had scattered through the house, so she and Ralph were left with the task. She at one end and Ralph at the other, taking hold of the metal rings attached at the ends of the door. The door needed to be lifted sufficiently so that the rings could be fitted into hooks in the wall. This slab of Douglas fir with its metal fittings was safe to walk over when closed, but not designed for easy use.

How could anyone open this door alone?

"Be sure to close the door once I am down the stairs. We don't want it left open," Ralph called up from the bottom. "I see a door to the outside. I'll use that one to get out."

"Hope I can do it by myself," she shouted down to him. "This is not a very good system."

No one was there to help. She unhooked the first metal ring by pushing the door closer to the wall then quickly stepped to the other end of the opening to unhook the second ring. Once the second ring was free, her grip weakened. The weight of the door became too much, and fearing that she might lose her balance and fall, she let go. The door dropped with a huge bang.

The buyers and their relatives were going hither and yon through the house. She decided to continue her inspection outside and let them enjoy an unsupervised look to discover any previously hidden or unknown aspects.

"Are you the real estate lady who's selling the house?" asked a small brown figure from the corner of the driveway.

"I think that house has lots of problems," remarked this singular-looking woman. Her face was like one of the shriveled apples hanging from the tree in back. Her hands and arms protruding an unshapely sweater had the same juiceless quality.

"What makes you say that?"

"Oh, I don't know. Since Rosalinda died, the house's been falling apart."

"If my clients buy it, I'm sure they'll fix what needs to be fixed—nice talking to you. Take care."

That's neighbors for you. They always have something bad to say about every property but their own.

Having completed her outside inspection, she went back inside. She followed the sound of voices and entered the enclosed sun porch where everyone had gathered to discuss Ralph's inspection. The porch was crowded. She took a step back from the group. As she did so, she experienced a sublime feeling, much like gliding through water. She felt her hair fly up and the papers she was holding being released from her hand. This feeling lasted less than a second before her fall was broken by the stairs, causing her to keep tumbling down. She was conscious enough to remember a brick post at the bottom.

Will I stop before colliding with that post? And if not, will that collision be painful?

"Don't move! Stay right there! The rest of you don't come down!" This was Ralph commanding. She was not going to move until she cleared her head. She had stopped before hitting the bottom. That itself was a relief.

She knew she had closed the trap door. *How did the door get open? Who had opened the door?* Nothing ached or hurt. Everyone looked at her in amazement as she walked up the stairs. *How is it possible that I haven't been hurt? That's fifteen feet down at least!*

"Who opened that door again? I know I closed it."

"Not me."

"I didn't."

No one confessed!

Theresa had collected the forms that flew out of Ingrid's hand and gave them, very carefully, back to her. "Are you really okay? Your hair went flying up. You really looked surprised."

"You must be in terrific shape. I'll put you on my team anytime," was John's only comment.

Ralph said nothing. He walked over to the trap door and went through the same procedure she had gone through to shut it, unhinging first one side and then the other. No one helped him. And, as before, there was a loud bang when the door dropped. His gaze shifted from person to person as he reminded them they would receive the inspection report via email.

Was he trying to discern culpability?

"Thanks for your business," he said. "You can call me if you want more information."

They locked the doors, said their good-byes—something strange hung over the departure. *What wasn't being said?*

On her way out of town, she stopped at Anna's office to drop off the house key. She told Anna what had happened. "Are you sure you aren't hurt? Shouldn't you see a doctor before driving home? I know I should have let that listing go."

"Thanks, Anna, I think I'm okay. I just feel sort of peculiar, like something significant just happened, but I can't put my finger on it."

As she traveled up the canyon out of town, her thoughts wandered. She tried to recapture how the momentary weightlessness had felt, how strange everyone looked as she walked up the stairs unhurt, the other agent's shock and dismay when she heard about the fall. Her dream came to mind. She had fallen down a rectangular opening without being hurt, just like the dog ended up at the bottom of the rectangular pool without drowning. Had her dream been a premonition that had prepared her, thereby softening the fall? Did she know she was going to be all right and consequently felt no fear as she tumbled down?

SOME WEEKS LATER, John stopped by her office. He and
Theresa had come to town to see a doctor. They wanted to
say hello and let her know Theresa had also fallen down the
trap door. Theresa was in the car, too badly hurt in the fall
to come in.

Ingrid went outside and found her client with a black
eye and swollen lips sitting in the back seat unable to move
without pain.

"Theresa, how did this happen?"

"Well, I'm not sure. I was using the old wringer washer to
do some laundry 'cause the new appliances hadn't come yet.
I kinda like pushing the washed clothes through the wringer
and pulling them out at the other end all flat and scrunched
up. The sun porch works real good and dries everything
fast. That's exactly what I did this morning. The last sheet
I pushed and pulled through was pretty big, so I started to
step around the back of the machine so I could pull a little
better. The clothes basket was in the way, and I had to step
around it. All of a sudden, my feet left the floor, didn't touch
anything, and I was tumblin' down the basement steps."

"Had you opened the trap door?"

"I really don't remember if I did or didn't. John helped
me open it earlier to get the laundry basket and detergent
up, but I thought we closed it again. I could almost swear
that we did!"

"Theresa, I told you we closed it, and there was nobody
else in the house but you and me."

"I'm not sure nobody else is there. Sometimes at night,
when we're watching TV, I think I smell popcorn being

made. Like someone's in the kitchen. I don't smell it so much anymore, but just now and then."

As Ingrid listened to the two, she felt a chill come over her.

"Well, once we get home, I'm going to nail that door shut, and it'll stay shut as long as I own that house," declared John with considerable vehemence.

I hope so!

CHAPTER 7

PATRICK

"Guess who's coming. Do we have any of that spray left?"

"Not sure—maybe we should buy some on our way to lunch."

"Oh, *Martha Stewart*, you have a customer coming."

One of them must have spotted Patrick on his bicycle heading here.

The comings and goings in the busy intersection were clearly visible from the many windows of the real estate office. This was usually an advantage, but today she had been too busy to notice Patrick's approach. Now all of the other agents were taking off, leaving her alone in the office.

How annoyed everyone seemed to get when he came, how disgusting his smell was to them, all the while claiming how sorry they were that things weren't better for him. *It's not as though he comes often. Weeks go by before he appears. Sure, sometimes it's only a matter of a day or two—so what?* She was relieved when he didn't come, but then would get a little worried. *Did he get run over? Was his bicycle stolen? Was he sick?*

True enough, the smell of damp earth and alcohol preceded him when he opened the door. She always tried to gauge which smell dominated. If the smell of earth was more powerful, then there would be decent conversation. If the smell of alcohol lingered longer, then the discussions would be rambling and bizarre. He would claim he had traveled with the Rolling Stones or he had a connection with the Beatles.

"That Keith Richards was something else. Man did we spend some crazy times together. But when it comes to the guitar, man, there was and never will be anyone better!"

"What group does he play for, or did he play for?"

"Are you serious?" He questioned her in total amazement. "Don't you know? The Rolling Stones, of course. Haven't you heard *You Can't Get No [Satisfaction]?*"

"Patrick, the last time I paid attention to rock 'n' roll was when Elvis Presley was young."

Again, a look of amazement crossed his face. He almost looked sad. His disappointment in her, or so it seemed, was enormous.

Or, he would tell her of his various artistic accomplishments. "I used to work a lot with oil paint on huge canvases, but the lead in the paint damaged my liver. The alcohol didn't help either."

"Have you tried some of the new paint? I don't think they put lead in the paint anymore."

When he couldn't or didn't want to continue in the direction the conversation was going, he would simply sit and look at her and eventually say, "Got to go now. Let me know when something new comes on the market."

"Oh, do you have a phone now?"

"Nope, I'll call you."

He was always going to make something for her to show off his talent. What that was she could never decipher. In the end, she never received anything.

At times he would interrupt himself while talking and look at her intently. She wondered if he was trying to understand who she was and how he found himself sitting beside her desk. Perhaps he was trying to achieve some clarity of thought or simply get a clearer physical image of her. After such pauses, he would announce with certainty, as though he had had an epiphany, "You know, you look just like Martha Stewart."

The first time he told her she resembled Martha Stewart she wondered how he was even aware of Martha Stewart— Martha Stewart, the doyenne of all home improvement gurus! She couldn't imagine him reading a Martha Stewart home improvement magazine or cookbook while settling into the earth near a freeway overpass or stretching out in a deserted building. The rare occasion when he might be able to indulge in a motel room and watch television, he surely would not choose Martha Stewart's program. But then, one should never underestimate a potential "customer's" interests or past.

His visits, although erratic, had begun when he got word that his grandmother had died and willed him a small sum of money. He wanted to be sure to have selected a property before the settlement came so that when he received the money it would immediately go into escrow for the purchase. There would then be no chance to spend it foolishly.

"I don't want to be walking around with all that money. Could I have them send the check to you?"

"No, that wouldn't be a good idea, Patrick. If you are staying around here, why don't you get a P.O. box or get a bank account and have them direct deposit the money? It's not a good idea for me to handle any of your money directly."

He wanted acreage, a little removed from town with lots of privacy and room to roam—trees would be nice and maybe a little stream or creek flowing through and maybe a nice view of Mt. Shasta. If it had a little cabin on it, that would be nice, but not necessary. In essence, he wanted what a lot people want when they dream of living in the country.

So he would come in from time to time asking for possible new listings with these parameters. Sometimes she had new listings and maps to give him, sometimes he would just sit and talk in a distracted way, showing a little disappointment that nothing new seemed to be coming on the market. How he managed to locate the properties on his own she wasn't sure. He never asked her for directions or a showing.

His nose dripped constantly. At first she hesitated to offer him tissues, but when the drip became a stream, she couldn't hold back. He would take the tissues, rarely using them, crumbling them into small white balls he stuffed into his coat pockets—for later and better use?

The day the other agents all left to buy room-sanitizing spray, a new listing, not too far from the real estate office, had shown up on the Multiple Listing Service hotline—forty acres off a county maintained road at about 3,500 feet in elevation with electricity close by should he ever want to develop the property as a homesite.

He couldn't wait to explore this potential. Map in hand he left the office anxious to find the parcel, and she, relieved not to be asked to show the land, settled back into her afternoon routine, mildly disgusted with the returning agents, cans in hand, dancing around the room spraying every possible surface Patrick might have touched, mockingly declaring that this was what the "real" Martha Stewart would do under the same circumstances.

"Sure, make fun," she told them. "But you never know what the future holds for any of us."

Fall passed into winter without a sign of Patrick. Most likely, the forty acres they last talked about had not been ideal either. *Oh well, he will come or call when it suits him.*

On the day he called, it had snowed the night before—not much, but enough to make the roads a little treacherous and making it a little more difficult for those living in the hills to come to town. No worries for her this winter. She had bought a SUV 4-wheel drive for just such a time as this. The vehicle was *de rigueur* for real estate agents in that part of California—automatic everything, surround sound, navigational tools, and the most beautiful leather seats imaginable. She had not let herself be intimidated by the latest anti-SUV propaganda coming from Southern California where no one ever saw a snowflake or had to drive in difficult terrain. This vehicle was her gateway to independence no matter what time of year or place.

When Patrick called to ask her to show him the forty acres, she panicked. Her beautiful car! How could she possibly drive him up that impossible road! Not just the road, but the thought of Patrick's close proximity to her leather seats made her shudder.

Conscience and personal honor were at stake. After all, her mantra had always been that everyone deserved at least one personal showing. And since Patrick had never asked her to show him any of the other properties, this was his "one" time. She agreed to drive him to the property provided it didn't snow heavily that evening.

She woke up to sunshine and slush and the sinking thought of Patrick and her SUV. 1:00 p.m. was the time they were to meet at the office, and she would drive him to the property. At exactly one o'clock he called.

"Oh, Martha Stewart you are wanted on the phone," called out one of the agents.

He has probably changed his mind. "Patrick is that you?" she asked hopefully.

"Can you meet me at the car lot at the north end of town? I just bought a used truck. My money came in."

"Sure, I'll be there shortly." *Why did he buy a truck? Does he even have a driver's license?"*

Driving into the car lot, she saw Patrick standing alongside a rather used green pickup looking extraordinarily happy. She wanted to ask him all types of questions about the purchase—price, condition of the vehicle, was he sure this was how he wanted to spend his money, could he get a license, etc., but limited herself to, "Patrick, why did you buy this truck?"

For a moment it seemed as though he was not going to answer, "I thought you'd feel more comfortable taking me to the property in my truck. That way you won't get your new car all dirty. Besides, it'll be a good thing to have once I buy the acreage. You're going to have to drive. I still don't have a license." She panicked. This was a stick shift and she hadn't driven one of those since her VW bug ownership in college. Would her liability insurance cover this—was she even allowed to drive a customer's vehicle—what would her broker say to all of this?

"Patrick, is this truck insured? Is the temporary license sufficient to take the truck on the road? This is not a four-wheel drive, how are we going to get up there without that?"

Patrick looked at her as though he hadn't heard any of her concerns. "I know you can get us up there."

"I'm not so sure. The roads into that property never get plowed."

My clients always seem to ask me to do things that they themselves wouldn't do and then tell me, "Sure, you can do it."

The drive up wasn't so bad. The truck's back end slid a little, but nothing too serious. She stopped the truck when she saw a little pink plastic ribbon hanging from the lower branch of an evergreen. This might be the beginning of the property—no other markers were visible, however, and the heavy snow among the trees prevented them from walking any distance. It really didn't matter to Patrick. He was sure this was *his* his acres and once the snow was gone he would locate the corner pins. This Christmas scene of woods and snow and icicles, light blue sky and endless views of the valley below, was precisely what he had been wanting.

The wonderful smell of fresh snow and evergreens! Yes, even she was certain that he would be able to purchase this acreage.

"Patrick, let's go. It looks like it might begin to snow again. The sun's disappeared and the clouds are hanging very low."

"Sure, no *problema*. Isn't that the most beautiful place you've ever seen?"

"But how are you going to live up here?"

"I have a plan."

She was worried about the drive down the hill and forgot to ask him about his plan.

The trip home was a nightmare. No matter how slowly she rounded the bends in the road, the back end of the pickup felt like it was spinning out. She didn't dare put on the brakes too forcefully. She tried shifting down, but was never sure what gear she ended up using. The truck seemed to have a mind of its own as it glided down—ever a bit faster. Her hands began to ache she was holding the wheel so tightly. Her mind went blank. They got to the bottom of the hill by "the grace of God" alone. Neither she nor Patrick was meant to die or get injured that day.

Patrick did purchase the forty acres once the survey stakes were located. Whether or not he got a driver license, she never knew. Her only contact with him after the escrow closed was through a police officer who called several months after the sale to verify that Patrick was the legal owner of the property on which he was camped.

FOUR OR FIVE years after that sale, about the same time of year when Patrick had bought his property, she started thinking about him again. Every day her mind wandered to his disheveled person wondering if he was still on the property and how he had managed getting up and down in the winter. She couldn't shake the thought of him for several weeks. Somehow even the smell of him hung in the air.

"Julia is calling for you." *Who is Julia?* At the other end of the line was a woman who identified herself as Patrick's sister. Patrick had been found dead on the property a month earlier by a hiker. Julia called because she remembered her name from letters Patrick wrote in which he mentioned how helpful and kind his realtor had been in his search for the perfect property. Julia now needed a realtor to give a Broker's Price Opinion on the value of the land for estate settlement purposes.

Yes, of course she would do that. There would be no charge. She hesitated, but then decided to ask Julia to tell her a little about Patrick—that is if she, Julia, felt comfortable doing that. Did he really associate with the Rolling Stones and the Beatles and did she, Julia, possess any of his artwork?

"I can't think about this right now. Let me get back to you another time."

A few days later, she received an email from Patrick's sister. "My brother was true to his Irish heritage and had the charm and blarney that went with it. He was the third child of five, never married or had children. My older brother Daniel passed away before Pat, and I am the second oldest. Our mother and father were very involved in the Catholic Church and sent us to Catholic schools. Our father was a well-known attorney and became a judge in the '60s before he died. Pat was a free spirit from very young and traveled all over. He may have had some connection to rock bands, but I never really knew of any. He would draw and write to me, but I also never knew of any serious art. I miss him and will always love him."

She completed the market analysis of Patrick's property, typed the information on her company stationery, put the letter in a company envelope, sealed and addressed it.

She walked to the firm's outgoing mailbox to deposit the letter. She paused—a feeling tugged at her, and she lingered a bit before sliding the envelope into the appropriate slot.

As she walked back to her desk, she glanced outside. The sky promised more snow.

CHAPTER 8

IT WASN'T HER TIME YET

She was not meant to die, it wasn't her time yet. There could be no other explanation for several bizarre events that followed her through 2008. It was, however, an even-numbered year. She was sure the odd-numbered years brought her better luck and she needed to be especially careful during even-numbered years. For example, she was married in 1974, an unlucky year. Her son was born in 1977, her daughter in 1985, two very lucky years.

In addition to the odd *vs.* even year dilemma, a personality test she had taken hoping to discover her career interests and aptitude indicated, among other traits, she was more accident-prone than the average person. Having personality traits that predispose to accidents was as mystifying as the pronouncements by two psychics that she would have a long life.

She, just as everyone else she knew, had accidents, but what was an average number of accidents per individual in a lifetime? And what constitutes a long life—eighty, ninety, one hundred years? Well into middle age Ingrid Fromm considered herself healthy, no pills, no injections, no transfusions, and no dietary restrictions. By all actuary tables, she still had fifteen to twenty years of life ahead, baring her better than average accident proneness.

January and February 2008 were snowy, wet, and messy. The days ended early. Everyone was locked into houses for longer periods. Ingrid couldn't tolerate those long dark winter afternoons and evenings. No matter what time of day, her need for movement compelled her to brave the elements and shadowy nights. At about 8:00 p.m. on a February evening, she put on her snow boots, parka, old wool hat, wrapped a scarf around her neck, found her umbrella, and headed out from home.

She was sure her daughter Ellie would have been aghast had she seen this attire. She could almost hear Ellie's voice, "Mom, don't you have anything better to wear? Why do you go around like that? You really don't need to look like the local bag lady." At that hour and with those weather conditions, the streets would be deserted. No embarrassment likely from a chance meeting with that allusive, handsome stranger.

She would follow her usual around-town route—up Lane Street to Lange Way, north on Lange Way to Miner Street, down Miner to Gold Street, south on Gold, and then home. At the top of Miner Street, it began to rain, causing the remaining snow on tree branches to fall and land in heavy globs on the sidewalk. One lump of snow hit the back of her head and slid down her neck. She opened the umbrella, held it at a slight angle in front of her face and proceeded amiably down the slippery, slush-covered sidewalk. All was quiet, not a single vehicle or other pedestrian on the street.

She had almost completed her walk when the wonderful silence of the winter night was broken. She noticed a truck coming slowly up the street toward her then stop, almost directly opposite her, in front of one of the newer houses on the block. The driver got out and his passenger jumped out behind him. From Ingrid's location, the passenger resembled a bear cub, dark and lumbering. Walking slowly on, she noticed it was in fact an enormous hunting dog of sorts. The moment she recognized the animal for what it was, it also noticed her.

The driver slammed the car door shut and walked away, leaving the dog free to follow or not. For an instant, the dog stood still pointing his big head in her direction—nose forward, one front leg up and flexed. Ingrid liked dogs. She continued her normal pace along the sidewalk.

The driver entered one of the houses, the creature, however, had decided not to follow. Instead, he started to lurch forward snarling and yapping at Ingrid as it crossed the street. What was she to do? She knew she couldn't outrun it with or without her clumsy boots. Her vision was hindered by both the shawl and hat she had pushed down low on her forehead. She would most likely fall and be a perfect target for its canines. She could use the umbrella as a shield, but for how long? She stood frozen and senseless. Fear prevented her from calling out. *Didn't the owner of this ferocious creature hear the barking?*

The dog charged and was almost upon her. Now she could see the full extent of its fury—enormous yellowish teeth, brutal eyes, and hackles defining the ridge of its back. The end was near. Ingrid resolved to defend herself as well as she could with the soggy umbrella.

The animal, suddenly illuminated by car lights, was almost upon her when she heard a thud. The dog whimpered, turned, and ran to the other side of the street. Out of nowhere, or so it seemed, a car had appeared just as the dog leapt. The car hit the dog. She was saved.

The driver stopped the car and got out. He first checked the front bumper for possible damage, he then turned toward Ingrid, "That dog had it in for you. He was going to eat you alive."

"Yes, I think he couldn't quite recognize what he saw and was afraid. It might have been the combination of the umbrella and me that caused the confusion."

A front door opened across the street, a voice yelled, "Get on in here!" The door slammed shut. The driver and Ingrid looked at each other in amazement. *How had this man been so oblivious to what just happened?*

"I can't see too well, but I don't think the fender is damaged," remarked her rescuer. "Miss, you shouldn't be walking alone at night."

"I'll be okay. Thanks for your help."

It was no longer raining. The dog had been commanded

inside. The car and driver had left. Everything was quiet and peaceful again. She was almost home when a car slowed down alongside her and stopped. *Another car?* The driver rolled down the window on the passenger side, "Are you the lady who almost got attacked by the dog?"

"Yes, that's me. Why?"

"I'm the one who hit the dog. After I got home, I checked the bumper again, and sure enough, there's enough damage to put in an insurance claim. If I need you to verify what happened, would you do that? Could I have your name and telephone number?"

"Of course—you saved my life." She walked closer to the car. He turned on the interior lights. "Say, now you look familiar. Aren't you Ingrid Fromm? I'm Officer Black. I was the principal at the high school when your son was there. Now I teach police science classes at the community college."

Alex, her son, would probably have some sarcasm how apropos it was that Mr. Black was now an officer of the law. Alex always saw the high school as a type of prison and the principal its warden.

Amazing, so many years later to be helped by this now very handsome man—*age seems to treat men better*—who had called her to his office to discuss some of her son's shortcomings. *And now I look like a bag lady!* She could hear her daughter, "See, Mom."

Oh, well. At least I'm alive and unhurt. I guess it just wasn't her time to die yet.

THE ROAD FROM her new residential listing to its intersection with Highway 263 followed the Shasta River. And just like the river, it meandered gently, hugging the river's bank for guidance. There were no great twists or turns. The Shasta River is a new river. Older rivers curve more extremely and, in order to stay active, form oxbows; thereby, cutting off segments of the river and forming new channels. The deserted river channels become stagnant and eventually dry up enough allowing all types of vegetation to take hold. The new channels permit the rivers to right themselves. The flow of water becomes swift again.

Ingrid Fromm liked the idea of old and new rivers. She especially liked the idea of living near a young river, one that has not yet become bent with age or has cut off a part of itself, a cancerous wart, to keep moving. Her spirit rejoiced—this young, robust Shasta River flows steadily forward over farmland and under bridges, joining the Klamath River on its route to the Pacific Ocean.

Soon salmon will swim up the Shasta River to deposit their eggs in the sandbars. From the deck of her new listing, if the property has not sold, she will be able to watch the fish dig into the gravel with their fins before releasing the eggs. Hundreds of salmon pass by then disappear, their biological imperative fulfilled.

On this glorious autumn morning, she had time to enjoy a herd of deer grazing in a pasture. She stopped in the middle of the road for a quick look up to see eaglets in their nest perched high on the top branches of a huge pine tree. She drove slowly around a rattler heating itself one more time on the warmth of the asphalt, before slinking off into its den for a long sleep. She rolled down the car window to hear and smell the river. Too soon she would be in town again in her Yreka office, taking calls from clients who will ask her to explain and describe the county. How could she possibly relay what thousands of square miles are like to callers who think San Francisco is Northern California? It seems that most people, even those living in California, do not know that California extends over three hundred miles north of the City. She encouraged callers to come, visit, and investigate. But for most, Yreka is too far from the known.

She was almost to the highway. She had crossed the bridge spanning Yreka Creek, a tributary of the Shasta River. The comparison of a life to the flow of a river was certainly not a new thought, but she couldn't help herself. She marveled how symbolic of life these waterways are—Yreka Creek flows into the Shasta River, the Shasta in turn runs into the Klamath River, and finally, the Klamath River becomes a part of the vast Pacific Ocean. Just as the confluence of tributaries will determine the nature of a river, the confluence of events will help determine the character of a person and ultimately the destiny of the person.

The stop sign at the end of the road halted Ingrid's ruminations. Waiting for a semi to pass, she checked the glove box to see if she still had the newly purchased flashlight. She was to show a vacant house to clients eager to buy a "fixer upper." The electricity at the house was shut off. A flashlight would definitely be useful. The flashlight was there. Satisfied, she closed the glove box then looked to the left and right one more time before turning left onto Hwy 263.

Having completed the turn, she glanced in the rearview mirror. To her surprise, a greenish-looking Ford farm truck was inches from her back fender, stopping just short of rear-ending her car. Smoke was coming from all of its tires. She pulled a little ahead and stopped. She got out of her car and rushed to the truck to ask if she could be of help. There in the cab sat a middle-aged couple visibly stunned and frightened. The woman was looking ahead as if frozen in place. The driver, most likely her husband, had a white-knuckled grip on the steering wheel.

"Lady, this is your lucky day," was his angry comment as Ingrid approached. "God damn it! Didn't you see me when you pulled out?"

"I'm sorry, but I didn't."

"I had new brakes put on yesterday. That's the only thing that saved you from getting plowed."

"I'm sorry. I don't know how I could've missed seeing you. Are you okay?"

"I just about wet my pants—probably totally burned out the brakes. That's all!" He didn't look at her and retained his grip on the wheel.

"Sorry."

There was nothing else to say. She retreated to her car, sat there a while wondering how she could have missed seeing the truck. She had looked—at least twice before entering the intersection and had seen nothing. She could hear her son's voice, "After the age of sixty ..."

Her focus had been the semi, her thoughts on the next appointment. Could that have prevented her from noticing the smaller truck? Hard to say—all she was sure of was that she was still alive, it wasn't her time to die yet!

THE YEAR WAS coming quickly to a close. In a few days it would be Thanksgiving and then Christmas. New Year was next year's holiday—no need to worry about that yet. Thanksgiving was the holiday to think about now. For the first time in a number of years, *both* of Ingrid's children and their spouses were spending the holiday with her. She wanted everything to be perfect. She had cleaned the house top to bottom. No matter, her daughter, her most ardent critic, was sure to find that one corner she had forgotten to clean.

Was it her fault Ellie is such a fanatic about housekeeping? No, Ingrid was not going to take responsibility for that character trait. *Let her keep her own house the way she wants. My housekeeping suits me just fine. So there is a little spider by the washing machine, or a cricket hops around the kitchen floor, that's very companionable. Alex is almost as bad. Why does every book have to be in a bookcase? A book or magazine here or there creates a homey atmosphere. I don't have to search very long for the latest* New Yorker. *I know the exact pile it's in.*

She had read somewhere that certain genes skip a generation. That was it. Her children are much like their grandmother, her mother. She had to have everything just so—just so clean, just so organized. She was sure the Asians didn't invent the *feng shui* of placement, her mother did. She thought herself lucky to have escaped the curse of "just so."

This Thanksgiving weekend was going to be a wonderful celebration of gratitude. She was not going to cause her children discomfort. Every book was in a case, every magazine sorted by date—the older issues relegated to the garage— everything swept and washed. Even the cats would have to suffer some inconvenience. Their litter boxes and beds were moved from the laundry room to an inconspicuous place of the carport. One of spouses, she couldn't remember which one, was allergic to cat dander. The cats would have to be fed outside. Her daughter's dog, a mostly well trained pet, loved the taste and smell of the cats' exotic food.

She had researched the "in" foods and their preparation online. Vegetables were now roasted, not boiled or steamed. A new favorite, brussels sprouts, could be sautéed, but only in butter with a little olive oil. Margarine, once thought to be the more healthy choice, was now a forbidden fat. Turkey dressing was baked in a Dutch oven, not in the bird. For her vegetarian daughter-in-law, she was going to prepare walnut meatballs and an organic tomato basil sauce. Everyone else had consented to turkey as long as the turkey was free-range, antibiotic and hormone free. The dessert was to be dairy free, baked organic pears with chopped—not ground—organic hazelnuts, sitting in warmed almond milk.

Each was to bring his or her preferred beverage. This, she hoped, would eliminate any mistake she might make on that account. And so, her shopping list prepared, she began her trek over the Siskiyou Summit into Oregon. Medford, Oregon, the largest city within a fifty-mile radius of Yreka, California, was sure to have the right ingredients for this feast.

The day was overcast, but mild for late November. No snow or ice was predicted, a perfect day to shop in the no-sales-tax Oregon. Her car hummed along, climbed the Summit with ease and descended into the Rogue Valley without as much as a change in gear—the luxury of a powerful V8 engine.

The valley was winter-green. Emigrant Lake was full and broad, having benefited from the recent storms. Shifting her glance from the valley to the road, she noticed a bluish film covering the highway. Before her mind could register and comprehend the significance of this, her car slid out of control and whirled across both north-bound lanes.

Was she supposed to pump the brakes, turn the wheel in the opposite direction of the spin? She tried both. Neither worked. She no longer had control of the vehicle. It continued to hurl itself down the six percent grade—on one side, a thousand-foot drop-off into the valley, on the other side a cement highway divider. She glanced in the rearview mirror. Miraculously, the freeway was deserted. Spinning ever faster, she was alone in this drama. At last, the car straightened out, heading at sixty miles per hour toward the cement blocks. *How much is this going to hurt?*

The car halted as it smashed into the immovable barrier. For a moment she sat there wondering what she needed to do. Both airbags had ejected, causing a cloud of dust to fill the front seats. She imagined the dust to be smoke. At any moment the vehicle was going to explode. Panicking, she tried to open the driver-side door, but the impact had caused it to jam shut. She crawled over to the front passenger side and pried the door open enough to exit. Self-preservation is a powerful force.

Hours later, sitting in the cab of the tow truck that was bringing her back to Yreka, she realized how lucky she had been. No other cars were involved. She had come to a stop in the inside lane of a heavily trafficked highway which, according to the tow truck driver, is not advisable since trucks had a way of losing their brakes on steep descents. For a little while, this busy freeway had been deserted.

The Thanksgiving menu had to be replanned—no turkey dinner. A Thanksgiving brunch took its place. Ingrid had enough eggs at home to make a soufflé. The eggs were not exactly organic, but the label stated the chickens had more space to "stretch, perch, groom, and nest." Applesauce made from the fruit of her own never-sprayed apple trees and whole wheat muffins rounded out the meal. Not a particularly grand Thanksgiving meal, but then it had not been a particularly grand year.

Ingrid had escaped serious consequences from three life-threatening events. It wasn't her time to die yet. She looked forward to the coming year with confidence. It would be a stellar year, an odd-numbered year, a lucky year.

CHAPTER 9

A FOREIGN AFFAIR

"He's such a con man," her friend exclaimed with vehemence.

"Oh, I don't know," she countered. "I take a different view on that."

"Of course you do. You always take a different view."

The two women were used to meeting once or twice a week to exercise at the high school track in the afternoon, before going home. The rubber track provided a better surface for their aging legs, back, and feet than the cement sidewalks.

"Kathy, look at it this way. How often do any of us young or old or middle-aged ever get such outrageously wonderful compliments? He told me I was a 'fabulous, intelligent lady.'"

"Yeah, great! He also told you he was single, totally unattached, didn't even have a girlfriend. And didn't he tell you he'd end up living alone in the lakefront house he bought?" Kathy reminded her with more than just a hint of sarcasm in her voice.

"Yes, but he never suggested even the slightest impropriety. Well once, maybe? He wondered if it would be improper for him to ask me out to dinner. When I didn't answer he dropped the subject and we moved on to real estate matter."

"Well, what about the time he wanted you to meet him in the city to go over the paperwork you sent him?"

"But we never met. So what was the harm in that suggestion? I meet with customers all the time to discuss disclosures, contracts."

"If that's what you want to believe, okay by me. Just remember, I told you. He's a con man."

Kathy almost hissed the last phrase as she turned and walked off the high school track.

Ingrid, distressed by her friend's strong response, decided to do one more turn around the track alone. *So the man didn't tell me he was married. Married people do buy property in just their own name for many different reasons—tax implications, a spouse's poor credit score, separate inheritance, etc. He said he wouldn't bring a wife along. He did say he didn't have any girlfriends even though he had traveled all the way from San Francisco with a lady friend.*

Boris had explained to Ingrid that since he was such a

novice buyer, his friend, who had bought numerous properties, was along to give him advice.

Who am I to say who should come along with him? We're all in our sixties after all—what difference did it make?

Ingrid believed both men and women have a biological imperative that requires them to procreate. Once a couple has procreated, they are responsible for their progeny until adulthood. During the nurturing time span, father and mother should be faithful to each other in order to create the best environment for their children. An environment with adult disagreement, jealousy, and lies due to the unfaithfulness of the parents, is not healthy for the offspring. When the children have left home and established their own procreative environment, husband and wife are no longer required to maintain a united front. At this point, what does it really matter if people sleep with other partners when they are married? Couples can stay together for economic reasons or divorce without recrimination. They have fulfilled their duty to the human race.

Why profess eternal sexual faithfulness when all around us we are told to value sexual gratification no matter the age or circumstance of the individual? There is bound to be unhappiness when the biological needs in partners no longer coincide. Wouldn't it be more rewarding to move with your partner to another phase of consciousness—move together, or perhaps individually, towards spiritual fulfillment? Or at least agree to be finished with the "householder" stage, as the Hindus rightly named that period in adult life when men and women marry, have children, acquire property and the like. She thought this to be a reasonable approach to the boredom she saw in so many long-term couples.

This line of thinking continued to occupy her on the long drive to her next appointment. She didn't mind these country drives. As she cruised the beautiful expanse of the Shasta Valley, Mt. Shasta looming ahead, it gave her time to reflect.

But where am I, Ingrid, in this journey through life? Have I already left the sexual consciousness state and entered the spiritual plane or am I just plain stuck in the twilight zone?

Ingrid had also come to believe that life will give you whatever experience is most helpful for the evolution of your consciousness.

Has life offered me Boris Volkov as an experience?

He certainly was the most exotic man she'd ever met. He was born in a small Siberian town two years after the end of World War II to a Russian state official and his elementary schoolteacher wife. When Boris was twelve years old, his father was transferred to a Russian embassy in East Germany. There he attended a school set up for the children of the Russian occupiers and their families. Since the school had small classes, he received much attention from his teachers and earned numerous scholastic awards. A secondary benefit of living outside Russia was an improved diet. He grew taller and stronger almost immediately. Cossack, Mongol, Aleut, East European intellectual—all that implied the former Union of the Soviet Socialist Republics came to the fore.

As an adult he had marched in the Russian military, received advanced degrees in engineering and mathematics, and taught for seventeen years at an indistinct university in Moscow.

Boris was proud that the American government deemed his skills valuable; thereby, eliminating the long waiting period for entry into the U.S. He became a naturalized citizen as soon as it was legally possible.

His obvious intellectual abilities, which allowed him such easy access to the U.S., also gave him quick entry into Ingrid's sexual consciousness. For Ingrid, although she did not fully comprehend this, Boris's intellect was a huge attraction. Had she had more personal insight, she would have recognized that most of the men she had found desirable she also thought to be very smart—including her former husband. With Boris there was an added component—for a man his age, he was very physically fit and had a compelling, deep-throated Russian accent.

Boris, in his own way, was mystified by his relationships. "I never had any girlfriends. I just married the first girl I became acquainted with," he told Ingrid on numerous occasions. "After twelve years of marriage we were divorced. Again, I didn't have any girlfriends. I just married the next woman I met. If I had had sisters, I might not have married so quickly."

The reason for the hasty marriages was somewhat oblique, but Ingrid understood what he was trying to say—he liked the company of women and might not have married so quickly had he had the opportunity as a youth to be around females.

She had had similar thoughts—if she had grown up with brothers, she might have learned to be more comfortable around men and would have been wiser in her selection of a spouse.

Had Boris had sisters and had she had brothers, would their choices of spouses been different?

These two very mature people met, so to speak, when

Boris contacted Ingrid concerning a lakefront property she had posted online. Numerous emails followed asking her advice on this or that aspect of a purchase—home inspections, well and septic inspections, and the nature of the property's location.

A sort of friendship developed between them via these emails. For Ingrid, this type of friendship was a common phenomenon. For a short period of time, when there is mutual trust and respect between buyers or sellers and their real estate agent, a powerful bond develops. For Ingrid, developing this bond of trust was important.

She advised him not to make an offer until he had personally seen and investigated the property. He reluctantly conceded to make the 320-mile trip north.

"Ingrid, you look exactly as I thought you would," were his first words upon seeing her.

"Well, I hope the property meets your expectations," was all she could think to say.

They had agreed to meet at a fast-food restaurant near a convenient freeway off-ramp so he would not have to spend time locating her downtown office.

"Boris, leave your car here, I'll drive us to the lake."

"Good. Let me get some things out of the car and tell my friend to come over."

The friend was a nice looking middle-aged woman, a little on the rotund side, but with a pleasing smile. Ingrid later learned that this friend had been an actress on a television soap opera. She had come with Boris ostensibly to help him take an educated look at the property and advise him on the merits of such a purchase. She advised against the purchase—he bought the property.

His first project was to replace the roof on the workshop and the garage since both roofs were at the "end of their life" and, being wood shake roofs, a possible fire hazard in an area that was prone to wildfires. The garage roof was to be replaced with a red metal roof and the workshop with blue metal. His neighbors had advised him to use the same color for both, but the saleswoman at the home improvement center encouraged him to choose the colors that pleased him.

He told Ingrid that he had once visited a German village where the roof tiles were very colorful and whimsical, like a scene from the pages of a children's fairy tale. He wanted to recreate this memory. She mentioned something about this not being the best for resale, but that didn't seem to matter. So—blue and red it was.

As the project progressed, summer temperatures soared into the hundreds. Thunderstorms came and went. Boris's endurance and stamina were tested. (His original estimate had been no more than two weeks of work.) But his tenacity and growing relationship with the roofs made her think of *The Old Man and the Sea* as she read his emails.

Ingrid received his first email on July 10. "After a huge thunderstorm and a couple of rains—the Roof suffered … so did I … though as we all know Mother Nature never has a bad Weather, any Weather is a Grace … we should accept.

"Sending emails about the roof/work progress to people whom you like/respect is self-encouraging. The progress came to the slowest stage … though my work does move forward.

"The Roof … this demanding imagination creature, the mysterious, sometimes, capricious, but anyhow lovely lady with responsibility to keep me safe, dry and warm … when all around are wet, cold and even in great danger … those thunderstorms with lightning like from nuclear reactor splashes … already were here."

Ingrid felt sorry for him and stopped by several days later when she had real estate business in that area. She brought him bread and salt for good luck, an old German custom she had adopted whenever she visited a friend or acquaintance for the first time in a new home. When she mentioned the hope for good luck, he said he wasn't too sure about good luck.

He pointed to a couple of buckets and said, "There were many, many, many horseshoes nailed to the entry panels over the doors … currently repair of the roof required those signs of luck should be taken away at least temporarily. Two buckets of horseshoes. Ingrid, how do you like the unit of measurement for the horseshoes to be a 'bucket?' By the way, there were 132 horseshoes nailed to the panels … set in both directions … luck comes in, luck goes away. Maybe just sharing your luck with others should be a must, that's what the previous owner meant."

"Boris, why don't you hire some help? This is really too much work."

"I have had some help. Two of my neighbors, after a morning of drinking Budweisers, came over to help. This was much appreciated and I am honored."

"But this is really a huge project."

"Even one person can do a lot, especially if this person is I … maybe I am not being modest but truly I can … at least for now."

The weather continued on its blistering course. Ingrid received another email on July 22. This time he was reaching out to all of his friends in a group email.

"Yes my friends, though I justify my emailing as a way of encouraging myself to work ... anyway your spiritual support/advices are valuable, and of course, you are always welcome to come here in person and help ... you know what ... I think that a roof is an active alive creature. The Russian [roof] *krysha* is feminine word, that's right it is she ... maybe strangely ... but I feel so ... probably a fruit of a pure imagination after boiling in the hot weather brain gives up and only feelings left ... about the roof? I ask, would the roof like this or that ... 10 sheets of 8x4 5/8 inch plywood were substituted ... making the roof healthier, and looking younger ... and dressed in only plywood looking naked ... then the roof selected to dress in sort of underwear ... a layer of protection before the rain came again ...

"P.S. last time I felt tired like today around 45 years ago ... when I've been in military ... the roof wishes to get me completely exhausted ... though I have a nice ability to recover very quickly."

Ingrid couldn't help herself in her response to his personification of the roof. "Boris," she wrote, "this is the classic story of the old, sturdy, and very reliable lady being considered worn out and passé. But she exacts her pound of flesh and wears the master down in his efforts to replace her with the new and shiny. She hopes that the exertion of removing her will leave him worn out, unable to enjoy the pleasures of the new."

A quick response came the next day. "Wow!! Ingrid ... how poetic and romantic."

She had found his accounts of replacing the roof totally enjoyable, but wasn't sure how to interpret this last remark—was he being sarcastic? Were the emails too frequent and was there some undercurrent she didn't understand? She needed a sounding board—she needed down-to-earth, no-nonsense advice. Who else but Kathy could put these emails into proper perspective?

Ingrid had not mentioned the email exchanges to Kathy and Kathy had not asked about Boris during their walks. Finally, Ingrid couldn't contain herself any longer. And as they circled the high school track for the fifth time, she summoned her courage and summarized the email exchanges, adding that he commented how poetic and romantic her reply had been to his description of the roof.

"Are you still talking to that, you know what?"

"Well, he is really quite charming and he wants to take me to dinner in Ashland next time he's at the lake.

"I've decided to try out my new philosophy."

"Do what you want. Believe me! This is going to get messy! There's only one thing you don't have to worry about—you're not going to get pregnant."

"This might get messy or it might be fantastic! Oh Kathy, I've been such a straight arrow my entire life. As Boris would say in his somewhat distorted English, 'live life long, learn life long.'"

"Distorted, Ingrid? What the heck is he saying? It's all distorted."

The days before the scheduled rendezvous were extremely busy. All at once customers called to make appointments to view properties that had lingered months on the market. With just a momentary hesitation, Ingrid assured some out-of-town customers that she would be available on the weekend.

Why did I agree to these showings? Now I have to email Boris to cancel. Perhaps that's best. He might still have work to do on the roofs—more rain is in the forecast. Maybe fate is telling me something.

She emailed him to beg off—some other time might be best. No response from Boris.

A week went by and no word from him. Ingrid wasn't sure exactly how she felt.

If he doesn't have enough tenacity to pursue me, so be it. It might have been fun, different. I certainly didn't plan for all these customers to show up.

She finally did receive an email a week after the scheduled date. He had been laid up for several days because of a herniated disk and in extreme pain. The ibuprofen helped, but then he had to go back to San Francisco to finish a project. He would most likely be there until the end of September.

Guilt came easily to Ingrid. "Boris, why didn't you email me? I would have brought you some meals."

Again—no response!

Had she offended him? Was he having second thoughts about seeing her? She hadn't indicated she would never see him again, just that another time would be better.

Why was I born with so little comprehension of interpersonal relationships? Other women always seem to understand the dynamics of such situations—why can't I? I'm not even sure I want anything to happen. This is probably for the best.

Best or not, every time she opened her emails she would eagerly scan for Boris' address—and not seeing it, regret her poor decision to show properties that weekend. Her life seemed a series of wrong decisions.

But he did remember her. He and a male friend stopped

by her office on the way out to his property during the last week in September. He had seen her car parked in front of the office and thought she was in, but had missed her—she was out showing properties to a customer who wanted to use his own vehicle.

Shoot, I missed him again. Was I born under a black cloud? Why had I agreed to have lunch with that really boring buyer? This friendship is doomed for sure.

She emailed him—perhaps they could get together before he left again.

His response, "Yes, I'll let you know when most of my work here is done."

The weekend came and went without a word from him—just an email with two pictures of the finished roofs, no text.

On Monday she emailed him to say she was going out his way to look at a possible listing so she might stop by if he was still at the lake.

His response, "I got back to San Francisco very late Sunday night. I thought to call Saturday to go to Ashland ... it rained all day. Let's go to Ashland when I come again to the lake."

Ingrid had no idea how to proceed. Where was that famous feminine intuition that should have guided her? Kathy, she knew, would have had no hesitation. "That louse, Ingrid, don't let him treat you like that." Not realizing that her emotions had been engaged by this elusive man, thinking that her new philosophy put her on equal footing with any man, she barged ahead and emailed: "Boris, I was looking forward to seeing you again. How can a visit to Ashland be so impossible? It's not like planning a trip around the world."

Again, no response!

As the days went by, a feeling of "having been there and done that" engulfed her. *How many times have I come to this exact impasse? What do I really want from all of this?*

Kathy's comments on the situation during their most recent walk—"I told you he was no good. He's letting you do all the asking, that way he can tell his wife it wasn't his fault when she asks him about that credit card charge for an expensive dinner."

"Kathy, you always think the worst. Maybe he's sick again?"

But Ingrid herself wasn't convinced about the "sick again" possibility. These conversations with Kathy while walking around the track were becoming very depressing. She knew Kathy's husband had cheated on her and that their divorce had been acrimonious, but wouldn't Boris tell her directly that a social dinner together would not be possible?

"Ingrid, I don't think the worst all the time. Remember that Jim guy, the one who owns all those ranches and sent you all those text messages?"

"Of course I remember him. He had the nicest way of explaining his irrigation system to me."

"Ingrid, are you all there? You liked him because of that?"

"I know that sounds crazy, but yes, that impressed me. The tone of his voice was as though he was caressing me."

"So why didn't you answer his text messages?"

"I don't know, Kathy."

If I think hard enough, clarification will come to me. Boris is gone. It was not meant to be. Instead I'm going to write Jim about an idea I have. This time I'm going to get it right! I'm not going to hesitate.

Jim Rosetto had called Ingrid the previous year to see if she would take a look at his ranch and give him an idea of its value. He thought he might like to sell everything—retire from ranching, buy a recreational vehicle, travel for a time, and then decide where to live. His young wife had died unexpectedly, and he needed a complete change.

Ingrid had never met Jim, but knew of his reputation—he was litigious, not an easy type person. But the afternoon they had spent surveying his ranch had been extremely pleasant. He was a good-looking man in his late sixties—an older version of the "Marlboro" man in his sheepskin jacket, jeans and plaid shirt, cowboy boots, and Stetson hat. As he drove her around the two thousand acres, he explained certain landmarks and pointed out a location his wife had particularly liked. They had hoped to build a new house on a knoll that overlooked the entire ranch. The view from the living room would be spectacular—Mt. Shasta to the south and below them the hills and knolls of the Shasta Valley. Instead, he had taken his wife's ashes to the top of this knoll and let the wind carry and spread them over the acreage she had so dearly loved.

This sorrowful tale, told in a soft and even voice, played into Ingrid's romantic soul. Here was this rugged, often mean-spirited rancher (according to local gossip) showing such tenderness and caring.

The day at the ranch had gone well, but he had not listed his ranch for sale. He would send casual texts—asking about current market prices, letting her know he would be out of town (this she found somewhat peculiar), and sometimes, although rarely, asking her how she was.

Kathy was wrong. She did answer some of his texts when

he asked about real estate issues. She never answered any of the personal queries. In her fanciful outlook, that would have been almost sacrilegious. The man was obviously still grieving.

Outlooks do change. *It's been a while—maybe he'll answer my email. Why wouldn't he?*

During a slow Friday afternoon, with no one else in the office, she decided to initiate a correspondence with Jim Rosetto.

"Hi Jim,

"Do you remember we talked about taking trips and cruises when you drove me around the ranch. You talked about a singles cruise, but weren't really sure about that. I mentioned I had seen a program on TV about a cruise to the Arctic Circle—you thought that might be fun.

"A thought came to mind—why don't you and I plan a trip this summer to Norway? Take that cruise. Have fun!

"I know what I am suggesting might be somewhat odd considering we really don't know each other that well. Of course, you may be currently encumbered. And who knows what our situations will be six months down the road. Looking forward to your response.

"Best regards, Ingrid."

After hitting the send button, Ingrid wished she had not done so. There might be a slight chance some computer glitch occurred. No such luck! Within a week Jim sent her an email, not a text, this time. "Sure Ingrid, check back with me in May. The cruise would be fun if I'm not 'encumbered.'"

Shoot, why did I use that term encumbered? At least he didn't tell me to get lost!

To her surprise, on October 2 Ingrid received an email from Boris. "Ingrid I'll be next week at lake. Planning to prepare a couple of things for winter and maybe take my dear, which I paid for already Fish & Game (as you probably know I have a Life Time Hunting License) and dear tag for zone C now. We should meet—my back is much better, I do feel as a healthy creature again. Yours cordially, B."

Wow, what a surprise! Boris! Is there a Freudian slip "take my dear," "dear tag?" He's an avid hunter—is that an intentional mistake, a lack of knowledge of the English language?

But this small mistake took on a larger dimension than she knew. Her feelings for him changed. His English no longer seemed so charming—his expressions seemed old fashioned. In fact, whenever she thought of him, her mother would come to mind—similar accent, similar turn of phrase when translating sayings from her native language to English. Toward the end of her marriage, her former husband Brad also constantly reminded her of her mother. He, just as she, was quick to judge people and felt himself to be disadvantaged and unlucky.

I am not going there again. Charm is not enough. Mom was charming, also controlling, complaining, and unhappy. Good grief, no one knew how difficult Brad was at home. His public persona was that of a charming agreeable fellow—grinning at everyone he met as though they were his all-time best friends.

Now what was she to do?

Since Boris was coming from the lake and she from town, they agreed to meet at the only service station nearby—twenty minutes from the lake for him and twenty minutes from town for her. She would park her car at the station and they would travel in his car to Ashland. Before dinner, however, he had some items he needed for his fishing trip the following day.

Oh well, what does it matter—we have the entire afternoon and evening together.

There was a trip to Costco to buy the least expensive gasoline for his stay at the lake and his return trip to San Francisco. He explained that there was at least a one dollar difference in price between gasoline sold in Oregon and gasoline sold in California. He not only filled his tank, he filled the numerous cans he had in his trunk to give to his friends and family in San Francisco.

The afternoon dragged on—more stores to visit, more things to buy in the tax-free mecca of Oregon. The date finally ended—a peck on the cheek from him, a pat on the cheek from her.

On her drive home, Ingrid's thoughts kept coming back to what was to her particularly unsettling—*He didn't even get out of his car and walk me back to my car! It was so dark where I'd parked. Wait 'til I tell Kathy about this "date." I bet her first comment will be—"I told you so." Oh well, maybe Jim will text soon.*

CHAPTER 10

THE POETESS'S SHACK

It was June. The real estate market was quiet. Graduations, weddings, first-of-the-year camping trips, and baseball games took precedence. The office phone seldom rang. Ingrid Fromm had time to ruminate on the changing demographic of her "farm"—those 6,300 square miles (yes, 6,300 square miles) of Siskiyou County, California, in which she had lived and worked for the past twenty-five years.

A migratory phenomenon was taking place in this northern California county. The career-minded and the young were emigrating, and the middle-aged and the retired, or almost retired, were immigrating. What once were small family residences had now become the homes of single, middle-aged men and women. With few exceptions, the new settlers, filled with hope for the curative and inspirational powers of nature, were also looking for a more affordable lifestyle.

Among these newcomers was a sizable group of artists who had abandoned San Francisco to live in this frontier region of California. Here they had been able to buy homes with acreage for unbelievably low prices when the real estate market was ballooning everywhere else. Those who did not purchase in the countryside purchased old and abandoned buildings in the small towns, painted them in bright primary colors and set out to recreate the culture from which they came. Instead of grange dances and rodeos, they initiated storefront poetry readings and book signings by local authors new to the area. They established arts councils throughout the county and opened galleries to hold showings and lectures—a crusade to civilize the rube.

The monthly exhibit openings were a means for these mostly single men and women to meet and socialize. The shows attracted a small but growing number of the younger county residents who saw themselves as more modern, better informed, and more cultured than their elders. The young women, especially, were attracted to the worldliness of the single, middle-aged male artists, writers, and poets. The artists in turn were not shy in accepting the inspiration of the young. After all, every artist needs a muse.

Ingrid had helped a number of these immigrants find homes around the county. She enjoyed their company and found their more expansive lifestyles interesting. Perhaps she had been an artist in a previous life and would have been again if "this" life had not played out in such a convention-al way—marriage, children, divorce, real estate. Her more fanciful side liked to think so. She marveled sometimes how she, an immigrant herself, had managed to assimilate into this western frontier culture.

Eugene Gillman was her first artist client. She had no idea who he was, or what type of art was his forte when she met him while trying to locate a building lot in a place called Shasta Vista. Shasta Vista, some thirty miles southeast of Yreka, California, has the look and feel of high desert—sagebrush, junipers and lava rock from Mt. Shasta's past vol-canic activity. From every direction a majestic aspect of this volcano is visible—hence, the name Shasta Vista.

The afternoon she met Eugene, she had stopped her car in the middle of Martin Road, not wanting to disturb a rat-tler that was fully stretched out across the road sunning it-self. It was at least six feet long with an enormous viper head and a score of rattles on its tail. She hoped it would move on its own without her help. Ingrid had learned to use a long stick to move these critters along, but did not particularly like doing it. Her children, who without effort had picked up the dos and don'ts of rattlesnake country, had made a snake stick for her some years before. It had the appearance of a hiking staff, but was forked at one end. Her daughter had tied some jingle bells to the top. Snakes, hearing the bells, would slither away. In case snakes couldn't hear, as some scientists maintain, she was to use the forked end to pin its head to the ground, and then guide it away.

While debating what to do in this instance, a car stopped behind her. The driver got out and headed toward her. As he approached, she pointed to where the snake was lying. He stopped cold.

"It's okay, but don't come any closer," Ingrid said calmly as she got out of her own car. "I'm trying to decide how to move it. I don't like driving over a snake, even a rattler."

She decided to hurry up the process by throwing a couple of small rocks in the snake's direction. This was successful. The snake roused itself and slithered slowly and gracefully into a clump of rocks.

"I see, snakes haven't left the Garden of Eden yet," was his measured observation.

Garden of Eden! This guy is not from around here. No one thinks of Shasta Vista as a Garden of Eden. A rock quarry maybe, but certainly not a garden of any kind.

"By the way, my name is Ingrid Fromm. I'm a real estate agent. Would you be looking for real estate to buy?"

"I am. I'm Gene."

"Do you have an agent yet?"

"No, not yet. I might drive around some—see the lay of the land."

"Driving people around is my specialty, but it would be more productive if you could come to my office so I can give you a virtual tour of the properties that meet your requirements. Computers are great for that."

"I guess that would be the thing to do," he replied in the same measured tone as before.

Ingrid could almost hear the mental calculations going on in his head—*Was this the prudent thing to do? What type of real estate agent picks up clients on a deserted country road?*

They chatted a bit about the type of property he wanted, what amenities it should have, and how much he wanted to spend. They exchanged cards, and Ingrid promised to call in the next day or so with properties she thought might suit him.

Wow! This almost never happens. What timing! So much in life depends on the right place at the right time and, in this case, the right snake. I wonder if he will really come to the office when I call. Oh well, nothing ventured, nothing gained!

The office meeting was helpful. She learned more about his preferences and needs as an artist. They decided on several properties to view. The one that had caught his attention immediately was a former dairy with all types of outbuildings plus a huge metal milk barn with concrete flooring and electricity. This space would be very suitable for the type of sculptures he created—large metal pieces for outdoor places such as public parks, commercial buildings, etc.

The main house was a triple-wide mobile home with cathedral ceilings, an enormous amount of space for a single guy. The two additional mobile homes on the forty acres could be used for guest quarters or rentals. The property was vacant and bank owned.

They spent most of the following day looking at the properties on the list. The dairy was the last one to be viewed. She had put the dairy at the end of the tour hoping that Gene would like one of the other properties so well that there would be no need to show it. For Ingrid, the dairy brought to mind events and people best forgotten. She had to remind herself that she was in the business of selling real estate—not in the business of dispelling dreams.

None of the other properties interested him—she was obliged to show him the abandoned dairy. As they drove up the long rock-lined entry, she could tell that Gene was taken by the property. His enthusiasm increased as they walked around—he could do this and that with this and that building. The forty acres were a perfect buffer from neighbors.

"I want the property," he announced as they drove out through the arched gate with its upside down horseshoes.

"Do you want to think about it overnight?" she inquired hopefully.

"Nope, let's write an offer today. You have time, don't you?"

"Yes, I have time."

They discussed the price, water tests, septic and home inspections, and other items pertinent to a thoughtful offer. Ingrid was conducting two conversations driving back to the office—one with herself and the other with her client. Her private conversation was torturous. *Did Gene have the right to know about the previous owners if it really didn't affect his health or safety or the value of the property?* No person had died on the property, no illegal substances had been grown. But its recent history was not wholesome.

Six months earlier, the Bakers had lost the property through foreclosure proceedings. They had tried to sell the dairy on their own before Mr. Baker had been sent to jail, but were not successful.

Mrs. Baker, aware she did not have the ability to handle a sale on her own, hired a local agent from a national real estate franchise to list the property. Ingrid had a client who thought it would be suitable as a training facility and horse camp for adults. She and the client viewed the Bakers' property multiple times and each time walked away in total amazement. All of the bedrooms had cases of canned or packaged food items. The kitchen overflowed with groceries, enough items to supply a country market. A number of freezers lined the enclosed porch and the patio at the back of the mobile. In addition to food items, there were piles of clothes in every room, most of which still had store tags attached. This was hoarding on a grand scale!

On one of the trips to the property, they stumbled upon two dead goats in the dairy barn. An emaciated horse paced outside the barn trying to find a previously overlooked blade of grass. A couple of mice scurried into an empty, overturned milk can. None of this, however, seemed to bother her client who decided that this was the place for her. The client wrote an offer, but the jailbird husband refused it on the grounds that it was "insulting." Ingrid's client decided that fate had intervened and moved to Arizona.

Some months later, after the pending foreclosure notices were posted, Rose (Mrs. Baker) and her three children moved into a rental in Yreka.

Now Ingrid found herself again involved with this property. Although all evidence of the Bakers' stay had been removed, knowledge of the squalor and meanness of their lives weighed on Ingrid. *Should I tell Gene of Mr. Baker's hideous conduct? Would that influence his decision? Maybe he will also feel the karma surrounding the farm and change his mind.*

Eugene Gillman, however, did not change his mind. The property suited him, and he was thrilled at the thought of owning forty acres plus all of the attachments. He had never imagined himself a land baron and the thought excited him. He would have enough space to invite friends from the City for weekends of creative interaction enhanced by the mystic power of Mt. Shasta. Ingrid imagined his mind was dancing with endless sensual possibilities this property would inspire. *Who would see, and who would know?*

Once all the papers were signed, inspections made, escrow completed, Ingrid had no more reason to be in contact with Gene. She would write him a thank-you note and send him a small gift acknowledging gratitude for his business. Oddly enough, Rose Baker came into the office—just as Ingrid was deciding what to give Gene—to show off the gift baskets Rose made that could serve as housewarming presents for clients. *I bet the items in those baskets came from her old house.*

Although Ingrid felt some empathy for Rose—*but for the grace of God go I*—and Rose's need to support her children, she thought it might be bad luck for Gene if she gave him one of those baskets. Instead, she sent him a gift certificate for the most popular restaurant in the area. Gene was a bachelor and would most likely appreciate this more than Rose's gift basket.

It wasn't just Rose and her children she worried about, she also worried about Gene. She sometimes ran into him at art show openings, would chitchat with him and wonder if his hopes and dreams were being fulfilled. On such occasions he looked a little scruffier than when she first met him. He had grown a beard, and now sported a ponytail. His clothes were always rumpled. In fact, he always looked as though he had just tumbled out of bed.

During one of these occasions, she dared ask him how things were out in the country. "Gene, now that you have such a huge studio, have you been able to concentrate on producing larger sculptures?"

"Well, not really," was his curt reply.

"So, what are you working on?" she queried.

"The property needs a lot of work. I've been building more rock fences, getting rid of some rubble and, in general, just shaping things up. I can't work unless my surroundings are in order."

"I drive past your place every time I go up to Dorris or MacDoel. The other day I noticed a structure going up on the little knoll on your property that faces the county road."

"Yes. Just something I'm trying out," he said looking away from her.

"Looks like it has a great view of Mt. Shasta and the valley."

"Definitely!"

His reticence about the structure caused her to pay even closer attention. Sometimes there would be a flag flying near the front. She couldn't quite make out the images on the flag. It looked as though it was a Canadian flag with the red maple leaf on a white square in a field of red or perhaps a Turkish flag with the white star and crescent against the red. At any rate, it was red and white—in great contrast to the blue sky above.

When the flag was out, Ingrid imagined someone was visiting. When she could not see the flag, it indicated that the structure was unoccupied.

The image of this little building, sitting on a knoll looking south toward Mt. Shasta, would sometimes come into her consciousness for no specific reason. Her thoughts would then wander between the morbid and the wistful. At times the building invoked the romantic sentiment expressed in a nineteenth century German lyric poem by Heinrich Heine that tells of a fir tree standing alone on a barren hilltop in the north. The tree, covered with a blanket of snow and ice, dreams and longs for a palm tree, alone and silent, on a scorching hillside, in the land of the morning sun.

The darker and more peculiar images arise more frequently. Gene has become aware of the evil that possessed the dairy and built the shack with the idea of gathering up all of the bad spirits at the farm and putting them in this building under lock and key—the reverse of Pandora's Box. She hoped that Mr. Baker's demon spirit was already in there, locked up for all eternity. *How could a father so abuse his son that the boy had to be hospitalized for both physical and emotional trauma? How could he give his own son venereal disease? How could a mother stand by and allow all that to take place?* Should Rose be considered a victim or should she be locked up alongside her husband in Gene's shack? Ingrid couldn't quite make up her mind about that.

Although she hoped for Mr. Baker's eternal damnation, this little shack really didn't manifest an image of retribution—on the contrary, it stood out there for the world to see, more like a sculpture, or maybe, a beacon in the desert welcoming those travelers on Highway A-12.

For whom or for what had Gene constructed this shack? No matter, these idle speculations made the time pass more quickly as she traveled the long distances from one end of the county to the other.

Her cell phone rang, pulling her out of the most recent "shack revelry."

"Hi, this is Ingrid Fromm."

"Gene here. Got a minute?"

Gene ... Gene, why don't people tell me their last name? Now I'm going to have to figure out from the conversation which Gene it is. I can't ask, Gene who?

"Hi, Gene, what can I do for you? Let me pull over so I can hear."

"Should I call back later?"

"No, that's fine. I've pulled off the road."

"Great, I have a friend who's coming up in the next couple of days and might want to look at property. Would you have time to show him around? I told him you could probably find him something reasonably priced."

"Where's he coming from?"

"San Francisco. He and I used to share a studio."

San Francisco, studio … must be Gene Gilman. "Just call me when he's here. And Gene—thanks for the referral. I appreciate that."

Another artist—probably another middle-aged man with an eye for twenty-year-olds. As long as he has money to buy something, who cares? Who am I kidding, of course I care. What impact do all of these artists have on our economy? Seems like the county is getting poorer by the year. The natural resources we have, timber and mining, are off limits. Instead we have empty storefronts filled with art. This all has to lead to something—but what?

Ingrid pondered the unpredictable. No one knows the outcome of change. She understood that this might be some transitional period with the county shifting from agribusiness to art appreciation and art production. Perhaps there would be a new *raison d'etre* for small towns. *And how would I fit into this new life? Enough thinking!* Just better do her job and go with the flow. Change will happen with or without her.

Michael turned out to be a rather nice fellow, very talkative, gentlemanly. He had some cash to spend. He confessed that if he didn't spend his money now on property, he would probably not have it too long. He wanted something much smaller than Gene's property and he wanted to be closer to a town or city, preferably where there was a nice pub. He liked to spend his evenings with a group of companions. He really wasn't the country type, but since many of his friends were coming up North, and the homes looked affordable, he thought he might see what it was all about.

Gene had convinced him that life in Siskiyou County was becoming more agreeable as more of their compatriots moved in. Michael's area of preference was the town of Weed, some twenty miles south of Yreka. Weed had a junior college filled with country girls who looked healthy and pleasing, a couple of breweries, and pubs with congenial atmospheres. If Ingrid could find him an affordable property in Weed, he might be able to tolerate small town life.

And so the search began. It took almost a year. Michael was often gone for weeks at a time doing photo shoots with a video camera group out of San Francisco. He did much of the camera work and lent his voice for some of the narratives. A few times, Ingrid thought she had the perfect property for him, only to find that he was out of cell phone reach. When he did finally call back, the property was no longer available. As frustrating as it was for Ingrid, Michael took it in stride. If it happened it happened, if not, he was sure destiny had other plans for him.

Arizona, perhaps?

It was not Ingrid's nature to let destiny determine her paycheck. She doubled her efforts and eventually the stars aligned, the place was right, the price was right, and the timing perfect. Michael had just finished a big assignment and was going to be without work for several months, giving him time to make the repairs, renovations, etc. the property needed.

A year was sufficient to discover some of the character traits of a customer. Michael was not shy about discussing his various girlfriends. When Ingrid first met Michael, he told her he was now living in a rooming house. He had previously lived with his girlfriend, but he could no longer tolerate her monthly tirades and, since it was her place, he had to move out. Surprisingly enough, one of his motivations for getting his own house was his oldest daughter's pregnancy. He couldn't have his grandchild visit him in a boarding house, could he?

Ingrid's interest in art and artists subsided. She felt the urge to escape Siskiyou County. An overdue visit to her daughter in San Francisco was the ideal way to refresh her connection with the outside world. Driving into S.F. never confused her—it was the return trip north that caused her moments of panic. *Could this have some deeper psychologic implication?*

Her cell phone rang just as she came off the wrong exit. She pulled over and answered.

"Ingrid, did you try calling me? There's something wrong with my cell phone. I thought it might have been you."

"Michael is that you? Sounds like you. Your voice is so distinctive. No, it wasn't me," she replied. "But now that I have you on the phone, can you give me directions on how to get to I-5 north? I think I just took the wrong exit."

"I have no idea where you are. I really can't help," was his impatient reply.

"It's okay, I'll figure it out. Strange that you thought I was the one who called. If I can get myself out of this confusion, I might stop by your place on the way back home. I'm interested in the progress you've made on the house."

"Sure—stop by. It'll be good to see you."

Ingrid couldn't tell from his tone if he was still a little cross about her inability to navigate or his reluctance for a visit. But then, why did he think it was she who had called? *For once just go with the flow. Does any of it matter enough to speculate on motives sinister or otherwise?*

She managed to find her way to I-5 and relaxed. Approximately four hours later she pulled up in front of Michael's house. He came out of the garage, greeted her with charm and smiles, and a kiss on the forehead.

He showed her the improvements and explained some other changes he had in mind. They had tea together on the steps of the front porch and spent a long time discussing this and that about life in Siskiyou County.

She offered the opinion of how nice it was that he was able to move to an area where he already had a number of friends. He agreed. Ingrid mentioned that she had looked up Gene Gillman's web page and was amazed at all the awards and honors he received as a sculptor.

"He's pretty well-known in his field," Michael replied casually. "He makes these incredible metal chairs that really sell, but he doesn't want to make more because he thinks that's like artisan work and not really art—but then he's always complaining about not having any money."

Ingrid wasn't quite sure about the difference between artisan and art.

"The other thing about him, he's letting his place control his time. He's always working around the place and spending money on his various improvement projects. Right now he's building this shack. He calls it the poetess's shack."

"What in the world is a poetess's shack?"

"Well, it's a shack, a studio—some such thing. He is infatuated with a woman poet.

"Gene hopes that she'll visit and stay with him. She'll get a surge of inspiration looking at Mt. Shasta through a huge window on the south wall of the shack as she writes."

"Michael, that's a sweet notion. He wants to be her muse. Don't you think that's lovely and sincere?"

"Sincere and lovely, sure—what he doesn't know is that, if and when she comes, she's going to stay with me."

A romantic triangle, but not just the ordinary run-of-the-mill Siskiyou County "shuffle,"—but maybe it is. How is this going to turn out? Two artists in love with the same woman! I knew that building was significant. Gene wants to capture his love, not the old demons and horrors of the Bakers' stay at the farm. But then, why is he looking so terrible? Maybe it doesn't matter what the obsession is, obsession is not good for the spirit.

"Michael, do you think she will come?"

"Perhaps, can't tell right now."

"Poor Gene—I hope he won't be devastated if she doesn't come. Thanks for the story. I've been wondering about the shack."

"He'll get over it. He always does. Hey—if you want a little diversion, stop by again. I'm home most of the time or at the brewery pub."

Ingrid couldn't think how to reply. She gave a short good-bye and departed. *This is not a safe road to travel. He is a client or was a client. But then, I'm not a doctor or an attorney or a psychologist or a minister. I'm a real estate agent! As far as*

I know, there is no ethical constraint on my becoming friendly with a former client.

And so as always, the internal dialogue continued. Ingrid had heard of other agents getting sales in suspect ways. As she tried to remember who told her what about whom, the phone rang.

"Ingrid, Michael told me you did a great job finding him a place in Weed. When you're out my way, why don't you stop by so I can show you how the place has changed."

"Thanks. I'd like to see those changes." *Who in the world is that? Must be Gene, who else would mention Michael? Why don't people identify themselves? I know a lot of Michaels and Genes and Johns and Bryans. The time I had three Bill Smiths for clients at the same time things really became confusing!*

Gene's invitation to visit was not problematic—after all, he had a poetess for whom he was pining. Ingrid liked the idea of this romance and hoped the poetess would come, that she would write great and wonderful poems inspired by Gene's love and devotion and the magic of Mt. Shasta. Ingrid imagined herself to have played a small part in this romantic and literary success—never mind that she had hoped Gene wouldn't buy the property.

Weeks and then months went by. Rose Baker stopped at Ingrid's real estate office to tell everyone she was leaving the area. "Rose, what are you and the children going to do?"

"My mom died. She left me the house in Tucson. And she left it just to me—that's what the lawyer says anyways. If Frank ever gets outa jail, and I sure hope he don't, he can't say not'n about it. It's all mine."

Rose seemed to pull herself up a little straighter with this pronouncement.

"Is your boy coming with you?"

"Yup, I get to keep 'im."

And so, life went on—another spring. Ingrid continued to travel up and down the highways and byways of Siskiyou County. Each time she passed Gene's place, she looked up to see if there was a change in the shack's appearance. The mound of tumbleweeds surrounding the shack continued to grow. The siding on the upper portion of the little building was never finished. Was the flag getting tattered? She couldn't be sure. Had Gene's hope been realized?

Ingrid never visited either Gene or Michael. She occasionally saw their pictures in the local newspaper in connection with some art gallery opening or art council fundraising event. Michael seemed to have gotten involved in protest movements—no batch plants, no zoning changes, no mining, etc.

As other artists moved into the county, Ingrid resolved to accept the inevitable, the county was changing—the county was being pulled into the mainstream of modern America. The rugged sharpness of this California frontier was taking on the roundness of conformity, just as mountain peaks become rounded by the continually changing elements in the environment.

ABOUT THE AUTHOR

Ursula Bendix was born in Germany in 1945 and immigrated with her family to Portland, Oregon, when she was ten. After receiving her undergraduate degree from Portland State University, she joined the Peace Corps as an Educational Television Volunteer in Colombia, South America.

At the end of her two-year volunteer service she returned to Portland, completed her master's degree, and finished working on a secondary school teaching credential. She moved to Yreka, California, in 1976 and taught adult education and Spanish for College of the Siskiyous. She also taught at a polytechnic high school in southern Chile in 2018 as part of the English Opens Doors program sponsored by Chile's Ministry of Education and the United Nations.

She is owner/broker of Bendix Real Estate specializing in Siskiyou County properties for over twenty years. Bendix's *Land · Home · Mountain View* is her first short story collection.